# Rhythms of LOVE

## BEVERLY JENKINS
### ELAINE OVERTON

D0004124

KIMANI ROMANCE

To my good friend Regina Belle—Beverly

 KIMANI PRESS™

Recycling programs for this product may not exist in your area.

ISBN-13: 978-0-373-86160-6

RHYTHMS OF LOVE

Copyright © 2010 by Harlequin Books S.A.

The publisher acknowledges the copyright holders of the individual works as follows:

YOU SANG TO ME
Copyright © 2010 by Beverly Jenkins

BEATS OF MY HEART
Copyright © 2010 by Elaine Overton

www.kimanipress.com

Printed in U.S.A.

# You Sang to Me

"You're the only woman who's ever made me fly back like this."

"And I suppose you're looking for a reward," she said.

"Any bone will do."

Rising up on her toes, she kissed him, and it was all the incentive he needed to wrap her in his arms and drown.

They fed on each other with a lazy fervor that left them both breathless. He brushed slow heated lips over the warm scented skin of her neck and savored her soft gasps of response. As he blazed a meandering trail back to her lips, he knew that if he didn't make love to her sometime tonight he might explode.

---

# Beats of My Heart

Suddenly, he felt warm, gentle hands sliding over his rib cage as she pressed herself against his back.

Tristan felt his slow heartbeat begin to accelerate once again, as her busy fingers continued their exploration of his body. Using all the willpower he could muster, Tristan covered her hands to stop their slow progression, opened his eyes and looked at her beautiful reflection in the mirror.

As if sensing his question, Rayne said, "Tristan, I know what I'm doing. I want you."

## BEVERLY JENKINS

Beverly Jenkins is an award-winning African-American writer. She has lectured at such prestigious universities as Oberlin University, the University of Illinois and the University of Michigan. She speaks widely on both romance and nineteenth-century African-American history. Beverly was first published in 1994 and has published twenty-one novels. This is her first novella for Kimani Romance.

## ELAINE OVERTON

Elaine Overton resides in the Detroit area with her son. She attended a local business college before entering the military, and serving in the Gulf War. She is an administrative assistant, currently working for an automotive industry supplier. She is an active member of Romance Writers of America.

# CONTENTS

Dear Reader,

I hope you enjoy Reggie and Jamal's story. Although the school where she volunteered is fictional, the woman for whom the school was named was very real. Madame Sissieretta Jones was an icon of the late nineteenth and early twentieth century and sang all over the world. Billed as the Greatest Singer of Her Race, she was the first African-American woman to sing at Carnegie Hall. Although her name has been lost through time, she helped pave the way. In commemoration of Black Music Month this June, please honor her by learning more about her.

Thanks,

B


Dear Reader,

Thank you for taking the time to read *Beats of My Heart*. I hope you have enjoyed getting to know Tristan and Rayne. I love music and during the writing of this book, I swear I could almost hear Tristan's soulful voice in my ears! I hope you can hear it, as well.

*Beats of My Heart* is my first novella, so I hope I was successful in expressing the love between the main characters and the obstacles they had to overcome in order to be together. Please feel free to let me know what you think—my e-mail is Elaine@elaineoverton.com.

Elaine

# YOU SANG TO ME
## Beverly Jenkins

# *Chapter 1*

Regina, aka Reggie, Vaughn turned the key in her ten-year-old Escort and prayed the car would start. The plea was a daily ritual. The present state of her finances made replacing the aged vehicle impossible, so she relied on divine benevolence instead.

After two tries, the engine finally rumbled to life. The rusted green body shook and vibrated as if it was going to fly apart, but with her prayers answered, Regina backed down her grandmother's snow-lined driveway and headed off to her job at one of Detroit's most prestigious riverfront hotels.

She'd been on the hotel's staff for five years. Initially, she'd worked at the concierge desk, but when the economy hit bottom two years ago, so did the hospitality industry. Her position was eliminated, and it was either be laid off or take any opening the hotel had. She found a spot in housekeeping. It was good honest work and she made a point of doing it well. However, being downsized also meant bringing home a smaller paycheck, one that didn't pay enough to handle both her bills and college tuition, so finishing school had to wait. Having to withdraw had been disappointing, especially since she was just a few credits short of obtaining her bachelor's in Music Education. She wanted to become a music teacher. In her heart she knew her dreams would come true, but right now, she was just glad to have a job.

At the hotel, she parked in the employee lot and entered the building. Housekeeping was run out of a small office in the basement. Ms. Harold headed the operation and had been doing so for fourteen years.

As Reggie entered and punched in, Ms. Harold called out, "Morning, Reg."

"Hey, Ms. Harold. How are you?"

"I'd be better if Trina hadn't called in sick again. You'll have to cover her floors today. Sorry."

Reggie wanted to jump up and down and throw a tantrum at the idea of all the extra work, but because she was twenty-seven and not seven, she said simply, "Okay. I'll see you later." Sighing, she left Ms. Harold and headed off to start her day.

On the way to the room where the housekeepers changed out of street clothes and into their uniforms, she gave a wave to the waiters, valets and other service employees she passed. The hotel's underground hive was already up and running, and she felt good still being a member of such a dedicated and award-winning staff.

Trina, however, was another story. She was Reggie's best friend. They'd been close as sisters since fourth grade. Where Reggie's dream was to be a music teacher, Trina's was to become a beautician with her own shop. Reggie rooted for Trina's dream just like Trina rooted for Reggie's, but when it came to work outside of a beauty shop, Trina was not the most diligent employee.

Reggie entered the changing room, pulled on the shapeless

gray dress that was her uniform, buckled the shiny belt and went to grab one of the carts that held all the towels, bedding and other necessities she'd need to spend the next eight hours cleaning rooms.

Upstairs on the twenty-fifth floor, multi-award-winning music producer Jamal Reynolds checked himself out in the mirror. Tall and dark skinned, he knew he was a good-looking man, but that wasn't what drove his personality. The simple black turtleneck and black slacks were expensive but made him look casual and comfortable as opposed to the millionaire the music industry knew him to be. He preferred it that way. He wasn't into blinding people with bling or hanging so much gold around his neck that he had to walk bent over. His work was his focus and the only bling he cared about were the Grammys and Platinum awards he and his stable of artists displayed on the walls of their homes back in L.A. At present, he was on his way to a breakfast in conjunction with the fiftieth-anniversary celebration of Grady Records, one of the pioneering recording companies of R & B. At thirty-three, Jamal was too young to have grown up owning any of the Grady hits, but he and everyone else in the music business owed their careers to the tracks laid down fifty years ago by the great Charles Grady.

The hotel room's phone rang. It was the front desk informing him that his hired driver and town car were downstairs. Grabbing his bag, he quickly left the room.

He and the driver were just about to pull away from the hotel when Jamal realized he'd stupidly left his phone in the bathroom. Offering a quick apology to the driver, he hurried back inside.

A maid's cart was outside his room and the door was open. Not wanting to scare whoever might be inside, Jamal entered and called out, "Hello?"

In reply, he heard a woman singing an old Anita Baker classic in a voice so fine it stopped him cold. The pitch and intonation were perfect. The resonation, pure. His heart raced as it did when he heard a new talent, so he peeked into the bathroom and got the backside view of a woman in a shapeless gray dress on her knees cleaning the bathtub. Headphones were in her ears, and her voice was rising and falling as if it had been sent from heaven.

He listened intently. Not only did she have amazing range, but more often than not an untrained singer sang flat when wearing headphones and this woman was blowing. Fighting to keep the excitement out of his voice, he called a bit louder, "Excuse me? Miss?"

Singing away and in her own world, Reggie happened to look around and jumped, startled at the sight of the tall, good-looking man in the doorway. He was dressed in all black and the dark beauty of him almost knocked her over. All she could do was stare at how absolutely gorgeous he was. She finally shook her mind loose, hastily snatched off the headphones and got to her feet. She wasn't supposed to be plugged in while working and she prayed he wasn't a new member of the hotel's security detail.

"Um, I forgot my phone," he explained.

Relieved that he wasn't security, she asked, "May I see your room key, please?" No matter how cute, the rules came first.

He handed it over. As she walked to the open door and stuck the key card into the lock, she could feel his eyes on her. She tried to ignore the silent scrutiny but found herself peeking over at him just the same. The speculative amusement in his gaze made her hastily turn her attention back to the door.

Satisfied his key was legit, she handed it back, then reached into the pocket of her dress and withdrew his phone. She handed it over. "I already called security about finding it, so make sure you let the desk know you have it. I don't want them thinking I kept it."

"I will."

Reggie wondered why she couldn't seem to move. He had his phone and she had a roster full of rooms to take care of but they were staring at each other like two people caught in time.

"I heard you singing," he confessed.

"Please don't tell anyone. I'm not supposed to have headphones on, but it makes the day go faster."

"I understand. You have a great voice. My name's Jamal Reynolds."

"Nice to meet you."

"I'd like to talk to you, if I could."

"Concerning?"

"Getting you into a recording studio."

That broke the spell. She rolled her eyes. "Yeah, right. Nice meeting you, Mr. Reynolds. Have a good day." She moved back into the bathroom.

"No, wait. Here. Let me give you my card." He reached into his pocket and pulled out a platinum-engraved card holder.

"No, thank you."

"But I'm a producer."

"And I'm a maid with a bunch of rooms to do, so you go produce and I'll clean."

For a moment he appeared to be confused, as if he wasn't sure what to make of her. As if thinking maybe she wasn't getting it, he stated plainly, "I'm serious."

"So am I." Reggie knew better than to antagonize a guest, but the last thing she needed was to start her day having to fend off some joker intent upon Lord knew what. "Do I go back to work or do I call security?" she asked gently.

"So I can tell them you were singing when I came in?"

"Now you're threatening my job?"

He stiffened a bit. " No. I just want you to hear me out."

"And if I don't, you'll tattle like somebody in middle school?"

He stared. He didn't seem to like the sound of that. "Look, I'm Jamal Reynolds."

"You said that, but did you hear what I said?" she asked quietly and as politely as she could manage. "I don't have time to listen to whatever it is you think you're going to run on me, so just go, please, so I can get done in here."

He looked exasperated, then sighed. "Okay, you win. I'll leave, but I can make you a star."

"Uh-huh." She took the embossed card he was holding out, hoping it might speed up his departure.

"I fly back to L.A. tomorrow night," he said, looking all the world as if he couldn't believe she was actually turning down his offer. "Would you call me when you get off work, please?"

"Sure."

"Promise?"

"Sure."

"I'll be expecting your call."

"Okay, okay. Just go."

So he did, and as soon as he disappeared, Reggie tossed the fancy business card into her trash can and went back to cleaning his room so she could move on to the next one.

At the end of the long day, she pulled into her grandmother's driveway, turned off the engine and dropped her head wearily onto the steering wheel. *Lord, I'm tired,* she thought. Thanks to Trina not showing up, Reggie's normal eight-hour workday had been lengthened to ten. There'd be overtime pay in her next check as a result, but at the moment the prospect of the extra money wasn't enough to compensate her for the weariness plaguing every bone in her body. She'd made endless beds, cleaned endless bathtubs and vacuumed until her back begged for mercy. Now, all she wanted to do was crawl into a nice hot tub and soak until she turned into a raisin.

Inside the house, she found her pajama-clad grandmother chilling on the living-room sofa watching an old Western. Her long dreadlocks were piled neatly atop her head.

"Hey, Gram," she said with a warm smile.

"Hey, baby. You look whipped. Long day, huh?"

"Too long." Reggie plopped down into their worn green recliner. "Trina didn't show up again."

Gram looked over and smiled. "Good thing you love her so much."

"I know. Otherwise I'd be tempted to kick her butt for having to cover for her again. How was your day?"

"Mr. Baines and I spent the morning riding through the Pointes looking at the rich folks' homes. You should've seen the tulips on Lakeshore Drive. Absolutely beautiful."

Mr. Baines was Gram's current boo. They'd been together a few months but Gram wasn't sure how much longer the relationship would continue. Being a retired English teacher, she thrived on intelligent conversation and that was not one of Mr. Baines's strong suits. The Pointes, however, were a group of rich communities east of Detroit. You had to have large dollars to live there and the black families in the zip codes could be counted on one hand. Many Detroiters took pleasure in slowly driving past the big lakefront homes to look at the spring flowers, Halloween decorations and the lights hung during the Christmas holidays.

"What was Trina's excuse this time?"

Reggie shrugged. "Who knows? I tried calling her to see if maybe she was sick but I got her voice mail."

"Probably man related, knowing our Trina."

"Probably. I'll try her again later tonight." A book could be written about Trina and her adventurous love life. She changed her men as often as she changed her hairstyle.

"At least you have the day off tomorrow," Gram pointed out. "You can relax."

"A little bit. The kids and I are having the final concert rehearsal tomorrow. Any errands you need me to run for you before then?" Reggie was the volunteer music director for a neighborhood elementary school.

"Nope. Mr. Baines and I got groceries today, so I'm set."

"Good. Then I'm sleeping in."

"Pancakes when you get up."

"Deal," Reggie replied with a tired smile and got to her feet. "Oh, I met a guy today who said he wanted to put me in the studio."

"What kind of studio?"

"Music. Said he was a producer."

"Did he give you his name?"

"Jamal something. Started with an *R*...Reynolds, I think. He was in one of the rooms on my route today, or should I say, Trina's route. Gave me his card."

"And you said?"

"No, thanks."

Their eyes met. Reggie waited for her grandmother to reply, but when no words followed, Reggie planted a kiss on her cheek. "Thanks for not fussing. I'll see you later."

"Get some rest."

Upstairs, Reggie took her bath, came down to eat, then went back up to her room and booted up her old computer. She Googled Jamal Reynolds. The picture of him on his Web site matched the handsome man she'd met at the hotel, and his credentials were impeccable. He'd produced some of the world's most famous R & B artists; most of whom were her favorites. He had numerous Grammys to his name and, according to his profile, was single. Not that she cared. What mattered was that he hadn't lied to her about his identity, even though his truthfulness didn't change her decision to turn down his studio offer. *Once bitten, twice shy,* she said to herself. Her curiosity about Reynolds satisfied, she shut down the computer and crawled into bed.

She couldn't go to sleep right away though, because one side of her kept asking why she didn't take the man up on his offer. Especially now that she knew he was legit. At one time in her life, being a singer was all she'd wanted to be. Even after the tragic death of her mother, she'd kept her eyes on the prize. With her old boyfriend Kenny producing and writing for her, they'd hustled her basement-recorded CDs from Detroit to Chicago and Windsor and back, only to have a producer they were working with disappear into the night with a slew of Kenny's best songs and the three thousand dollars Reggie and Gram had scraped together to invest in demos the man said she needed. *Once bitten, twice shy,* she echoed. Her heart had been broken, dreams shattered. Deep down inside, a small spark continued to burn for the hopes she once had, but she refused to take such an emotional and financial risk again. She told herself sharing her love of music with the kids at the school was enough. Another plus was that as soon as she finished her degree, the school's directors promised to hire her full-time. But the voice inside that wanted her to reconsider going back into a studio wouldn't leave her alone. Finally, she fought it to a draw and slid into sleep.

Jamal thought about the singing maid for the rest of the day—through the breakfast he attended, through the hour-long seminar he gave at one of the local high schools and during the black-tie dinner held that evening to honor Charles Grady's life and vision.

When Jamal returned to the hotel, he hurried up to his

room to see if maybe she'd left a number on the phone, but there was nothing. Frustrated, he looked down at his watch and saw that it was past midnight. If she were going to call she would have done so by now. He also realized that he hadn't gotten her name. He called down to the desk and was told very politely that under no circumstances would the hotel reveal the names of its employees unless there was a complaint, and since Jamal didn't have one, he hung up.

He took off his tux coat and pulled the tie free. Removing the gold cuff links from the wrists of his snow-white shirt, he wondered if he'd ever see her again. It wasn't like him to be so driven after such a short encounter, but he was. Her phenomenal voice and attitude were more than enough to make her memorable but there was something else in the mix. He'd sensed chemistry, or had it been his imagination?

He hung his tux in the closet. Wearing a black silk undershirt and boxers, he padded barefoot over to the bed and climbed in. Picking up the remote from the nightstand, he turned on the flat screen and clicked through the channels. Nothing he saw held his interest, mainly because memories of the morning's encounter wouldn't leave him alone. What singer in her right mind would turn down Jamal Reynolds? he asked himself. Admittedly, he was a stranger and her skepticism was understandable, but his ego asked, how could she not know his name? Maybe she was what Marvin Gaye called a Sanctified Lady and didn't do popular music, but she'd been singing Anita Baker, so that couldn't be it. Whatever the reason he had to overcome it. The competitive producer inside didn't want her to be discovered by someone else, and the man inside was curious to know more about her.

He paused to watch Sports Center for a moment to check out the basketball scores, but her face came floating back, along with her sassy attitude. In his world, aspiring singers threw themselves at the feet of producers like himself, but not Ms. Maid.

He turned off the flat screen and stared into the darkness. Frankly, he'd never run into a situation like this one before and he wasn't really sure how to proceed.

# Chapter 2

Jamal awakened the next morning with a plan. He would be flying home that evening, but was scheduled to spend the day checking out some of the local recording studios Detroit was so famous for. He got on the phone and moved the studio appointments to later that afternoon. He was going to work from his room and wait for the singing maid. All he wanted was an opportunity to have an honest conversation and prove to her that he was all business. The music industry was filled with scam artists, but he wanted to reassure her his intentions were honorable.

But he had to see her again first, so with that in mind, he called room service and ordered breakfast.

The meal arrived a short while later. While he was enjoying it and looking over some of the lyrics one of his singers wanted on her next CD, a knock sounded on the door, followed by a cheery female voice calling out, "Housekeeping."

Taking in a deep breath, Jamal strode to the door and opened it.

"Morning," the unfamiliar woman standing on the other side said. She had short spiky brown hair, light skin and freckles.

For a moment he was caught off guard. "You're not her," Jamal heard himself say.

She blinked. "What?"

"Sorry. I was expecting the woman who was here yesterday."

"You mean Reggie?"

"Describe her."

"Brown skin. About five-three, ponytail, cute little body."

The description fit but to make sure he asked, "Does this Reggie sing?"

"Everybody in Detroit can sing, but girlfriend can *sang*, as we say here."

He smiled. "Do you know how I can get in touch with her?"

"Why?"

"I'm Jamal Reynolds, and—"

"The producer?" she asked excitedly. "I saw you on the BET Awards."

Jamal was glad somebody knew who he was.

"You want to produce Reg?"

"Maybe, but I need to talk to her."

"Hold on." She moved aside a stack of white towels piled neatly on the cleaning cart and took out a cell phone hidden beneath. "Do you mind if I come in?" she asked him while punching up a number and placing the phone against her ear. "Not supposed to be on the phone. I get caught one more time, Ms. Harold's going to fire me for sure."

Jamal, wondering how anyone could be so animated this early in the morning, stepped aside to let her in.

"She isn't answering." The woman listened for a few more silent seconds then ended the call. "Sorry."

"That's okay. Can I have her number?"

"No. You may be famous, but I don't know you like that."

He understood, and, truthfully, applauded her caution. "Can I ask your name?"

"Trina Maxwell."

"Nice to meet you, Ms. Maxwell."

"Same here. Does Reggie know how cute you are?" she asked slyly.

He laughed. "We didn't talk about that."

"And you didn't get her number either?"

"No. I did give her my card. She promised to call, but didn't."

"That's because no woman in her right mind keeps a promise to a stranger. You live in L.A.?"

"Yes."

Jamal was accustomed to women hitting on him, and he could see Trina sizing him up. "What's Reggie's real name?" he asked.

"Regina. Regina Vaughn."

"Will you let her know how serious I am? All I want to do is to put her in the studio, nothing more."

"You must be blind then, because girlfriend is gorgeous, even though she refuses to work it."

"No. Not blind. Just professional."

"Okay. I'll track her down and see if I can't hook you up. Just remember I get to carry her moneybags once she gets famous."

"Noted."

"Good. I'll come back and clean your room after you finish your breakfast. Ciao."

"Ciao." A pleased Jamal closed the door. He now had an ally.

Seated at the piano, Reggie stopped playing in the middle of the song and glared at the reason. "Shana Thomas, why are you singing with the sopranos?"

The nine-year-old tried to look defiant for a minute, but in the face of Reggie's obvious displeasure seemed to think better of that approach and looked away.

Reggie sighed. "How many times do we have to do this, girl? You have a beautiful alto voice, please use it the way you're supposed to."

"Yeah, you're making the rest of us sing flat," ten-year-old Alta Wayne snapped at Shana.

Grumbles sounded from the rest of the twenty-five-member choir of the Madame Sissieretta Jones Elementary School of Music. It was unanimous; Shana was getting on everybody's last nerve.

"Okay, settle down," she warned the grumblers.

Shana's twin, Shanice, gave her sister an impatient look. "Quit it, or I'm telling Mama."

*Good,* Reggie thought to herself. Mrs. Thomas wasn't going to be happy hearing that her joke-loving daughter was cutting up at rehearsal again.

"All right, let's start over." Reggie played the opening chords and the children raised their voices in the singing of "Peace Be Still." The sweet angelic tones filled the old gym and the purity gave Reggie goose bumps. They were fine-tuning the gospel concert scheduled for tomorrow evening. "Beautiful," she said quietly as she accompanied them.

Madame Sissieretta Jones, for whom the school was named, was one of the most famous singers of the nineteenth century and the first black woman to sing at Carnegie Hall. The staff's emphasis on academic excellence and music had resulted in much praise, but like most big-city schools, it struggled to pay its bills. There were infrastructure issues, too. The old building they were using was in dire need of a new furnace. The staff and parents hoped tomorrow's fundraising concert would help with the purchase of a new one.

The choir was in the middle of Kirk Franklin's "Brighter Day" when Reggie noticed Trina's quiet entrance into the gym. Trina waved and Reggie smiled in response, but the jaw-dropping sight of Jamal Reynolds entering on Trina's heels almost made Reggie lose her place on the piano keys. *How in the world?* Focusing on the faces of the kids in an effort to calm herself, she did her best to concentrate on the music and not on the tall, dark and handsome man standing by the door, but it was hard.

As the rehearsal continued, Jamal and Trina took seats on chairs positioned a short distance away from where the kids were practicing. Sitting quietly, an enthralled Jamal watched and listened. He couldn't decide which was more impressive, the voices of the choir or the musical skills of the woman seated at the piano. He knew her name now—Regina Vaughn. From a producer's point of view, the name had a good sound. Trina had described her as about five foot three, ponytail, cute little body, and that was in her favor, too. He could already envision her draped in a gorgeous gown on stage. He noted the flawless autumn-brown skin and ran his eyes over her erect posture at the piano. He could tell by the way she was beaming at the students that she loved what she was doing.

This wasn't what he'd expected when Trina invited him to tag along. She'd told him Regina volunteered at a school on her days off, and he assumed that meant in a custodial capacity. Was he ever wrong. He was blown away by her expertise on the keys and the way she directed the children's intonation and pace. Regina Vaughn was multifaceted; something else he found surprising. Where he came from people were about one thing—getting that break and making it to the top by any means necessary. No one he knew had ever volunteered their time to work with an elementary school's choir unless there was something in it for them, but that didn't appear to be the case here. She seemed genuinely enthused.

He also noted that after initially making eye contact with him upon his entrance she hadn't looked his way again, not even once. More accustomed to women clamoring for his attention, he was beginning to see that a man's ego was not Ms. Regina Vaughn's priority, and he kind of liked that. A rousing rendition of "Wade in the Water" ended the rehearsal. Before the children could disperse, Reggie stood and asked, "What time does the concert start tomorrow?"

Twenty-five kids answered as one. "Seven."

"And what time are you supposed to report to the music room?"

"Five-thirty."

She cupped her hand around her ear. "I didn't hear you."

Giggling, they shouted, "Five-thirty!"

"Great. I'll see you tomorrow. You sang like angels today."

The grinning kids grabbed up their coats and backpacks and headed out the door. Only after they were all gone did Reggie turn to Trina and Jamal. "Trina, can I talk to you outside for a minute?"

Trina told Jamal, "If she kills me, my flatirons go to my cousin down in Atlanta."

Reggie rolled her eyes. "Will you excuse us for a moment, Mr. Reynolds?"

He gave her a nod and she led Trina out into the hallway.

"What the hell are you doing with him?"

"He wanted to see you again, so I obliged. All he could talk about was you. Promised him I'd hook you two up."

"And suppose I don't want to be hooked up?"

"Do you know who he is?" Trina asked as if she couldn't believe they were even having this conversation.

And before Reggie could respond, Trina went on a two-minute tear, ticking off a verbal list of all the singers he'd worked with. "And that's just the folks I know about from reading *Essence* and *People*. Not only is the man gorgeous, but he really can make you a star, Reg."

Reggie sighed. "Trina, you know I don't want anything to do with the music business."

"I do," she said with sincerity, "but I also know that you're wasting what the good Lord gave you and it's gotta stop. Think how much you could do for Gram if you had some real cash to work with. Think about this school. You owe it to yourself to at least hear him out."

"No, I don't."

"Well, you're going to have to. It's not like you can snap your fingers and make him disappear." Trina's phone sounded and she fished in her big black tote until she found it. Opening it, she read the message and said to Reggie, "It's Brandon. He's outside." Brandon was Trina's current *man du jour* and owner of the building where she styled hair on the weekends.

While Reggie looked on, Trina texted him back a reply. Done, she looked up. "Gotta go. He's taking me to dinner."

"You're leaving?"

"Yep." Trina gave her a quick peck on the cheek, followed by "Love you," and hurried down the hall in her high-heeled boots toward the doors. "Keep an open mind!' she called back.

Reggie couldn't believe this. Outdone, she glanced back at the gym doorway and there he stood, dressed in all black and looking like a man out of *GQ* magazine.

"Guess it's just me and you, huh?"

His low-toned voice vibrated through her like a softly plucked bass string. His disarming smile didn't help. She fought to keep herself focused. "Did the two of you plan this?"

"Not that I know of."

Reggie understood that Trina thought she was doing the right thing by hooking this up but...

"I just want to talk to you, Ms. Vaughn. That's all."

"I thought you were flying back to L.A. today?"

"I am. Taking the red-eye."

He was persistent, she had to give him that. *Dark-chocolate gorgeous, too,* an inner voice crooned. She pushed that aside. It was also obvious that he wasn't going to go away until he had his say, so to hasten that, she said, "Okay. You can talk to me on the walk home."

"How about we take my car. It's out front."

"You're a stranger, Mr. Reynolds. We walk or we don't talk."

*Tough lady,* Jamal noted admiringly. She was right about him being a stranger, no getting around that. However, it was freezing outside. Being a Californian, he wasn't accustomed to temperatures in the twenties, and he was not looking forward to being out in the cold, even for a short walk. But to allay her fears, and to keep her from rescinding her offer, he agreed. "We walk."

"Fine. Let me get my coat."

Moments later she returned wearing a long blue down coat, a bulky knit hat and gloves. He had a coat, too, but it was lightweight cashmere, more suited for show than warmth, and it was in the town car. "Mind if I get my coat?"

"Nope." That said, she walked off down the hall toward the doors.

Shaking his head with amused amazement, Jamal hurried to catch up.

Jamal was freezing. So far, they'd only walked a short distance, but his feet in the fancy, black Italian tie-ups felt like blocks of ice. His hands and head were no better, and he got the distinct impression that she was enjoying his plight.

"So, talk," she said as they rounded a corner onto a dimly lit side street lined with houses that had older model cars parked out front.

"How long have you been with the school?" he asked. By the look she gave him it was obviously not the question she'd been anticipating.

"Almost two years."

"Not the question you were expecting?"

"No."

"Good. Keeping you off balance is probably my best shot."

"And why is that?" she asked, glad he wasn't finding this easy.

"Because you're different."

"Used to women falling all over you, are you?"

"Something like that."

"There'll be no falling here."

"Figuring that out."

They didn't need to look at each other to know they were both smiling.

He asked, "Do you enjoy being at the school?"

"I do. I'm hoping to finish my degree in Music so I can work there full-time."

Another surprise. "How close are you?"

"Eight more credits. I had to withdraw when I lost my job at the hotel desk. Housekeeping pays a whole lot less."

"Money from recording could help."

"True, but I'm not interested."

In spite of their not seeing eye to eye, walking beside her made Jamal feel like a kid in high school walking a honey home, although this honey was like no other. "Are you making this hard on purpose?"

"Yep."

"Why?"

"So you'll give up and go away, of course."

He threw up his hands.

She laughed.

Jamal couldn't believe how much he was enjoying her. "Woman, you are something."

"I'm just a chick from the east side of Detroit."

They'd stopped walking and were standing under a streetlight. She was looking up at him from beneath that knit hat, and he swore she had mischief in her eyes; there was a seriousness in them, too, as if she were trying to figure out who he really was. He told her softly, "I've never been turned down, and you're not going to be the first."

"Don't be so sure," came her softer reply.

In the drawn-out silence the urge to kiss her rose up in Jamal so fast and strong, it almost blazed past his defenses. Dragging his eyes away from the tempting curve of her lips, he stuck his hands in his pockets. "How much farther?"

"Just a little ways," she told him. "You might want to use the buttons on that coat before you freeze to death. This is Michigan, not a photo shoot." The front of his coat was open, revealing the black wool turtleneck, black sport coat and slacks beneath.

Shivering, he quipped, "Already there. Only thing missing is the undertaker."

While she looked on, he attempted to do up the buttons with fumbling frozen fingers.

"Where are your gloves?"

"Don't have any."

She shook her head. "Pitiful."

He chuckled and finally got the last button closed. In an instant, it made such a difference, he wished he'd done it earlier. "I'm new at this cold stuff. We never get this kind of weather in L.A."

"Here, it's as common as breathing."

"So I've noticed. How much farther?" he whined mockingly.

"Lord." She laughed in reply. "Come on. Almost there." She walked off.

In spite of her misgivings, Reggie decided she could probably like him if she let herself do so. He appeared to be on the up-and-up, and he had a sense of humor, but she had her life already planned out and it didn't include recording studios or a man who probably had women coming out of his ears.

"Trina said you two are best friends."

They were in stride once again.

"From the day we met at her mama's beauty shop. We even share a birthday. March 18."

"She thinks the world of you, and your voice."

Reggie went silent for a few moments. "I think the world of her, too. She thinks I'm wasting my gift."

"Please don't punch me, but I agree with her."

"That's because you don't know how much money I lost the last time I said yes to someone like you."

Even though Jamal was so cold he could no longer feel his ears, he stopped again and stared. "Trina never said anything about another producer."

"Good for her." And she struck out ahead of him.

Once again, he had to hurry to catch up, all the while wishing he was riding in the warm interior of the hired town car that was slowly trailing them. "When was this?"

"Ten years ago."

"Who was the producer?"

"Man named Wes Piper, or at least that was the name he used. One day he was there, the next night he was gone."

Jamal knew hundreds of people in the business but had never heard that name before. "How much did you lose?"

"Almost four grand. Most of which belonged to my grandmother."

He didn't know what to say, so for a while they walked on silently. "What if I offer to cover all expenses for demos and studio time?"

"No, thank you. I'm going to teach music."

"But—"

She stopped in front of a small brick house. Its bright porch light illuminated the front door, showing three small panes and the old-fashioned sitting porch. A beat-up green Escort was parked in the driveway. "This is where I live. Thanks for the company."

And, to his dismay, she slowly headed up the stairs. As she pulled open the outer storm door, he said, "Hey, wait."

She turned back.

"You didn't let me make much of a pitch." He watched her study him for a moment and again wished he knew what she was thinking.

When she finally spoke it was not what he'd been expecting. "Good night, Mr. Reynolds."

She disappeared inside.

Sighing his frustration, Jamal walked over to the car where the driver stood waiting beside the opened door, and got in. He'd never been so grateful for warmth. As the driver drove them away, Jamal realized this campaign to get her into the studio was going to be a whole lot harder than he'd initially thought, but at least he knew some of what he was up against. If and when he thawed out, he'd try to figure out what to do next.

Reggie watched the car drive away before she slid the shade

back in place. As she hung her coat in the closet, she freely admitted that both Jamal Reynolds and his offer were tempting but she wasn't risking her future on either one.

She found her grandmother in the kitchen washing collards at the sink. "Hey, Gram."

"Hey. How was the rehearsal?"

"Interesting."

"Meaning?"

Reggie told her about Reynolds's visit.

"You should have invited him in. I would have like to meet him."

"No, I shouldn't have. You want help with the washing?" Reggie hoped the question would change the subject. The greens were to be part of the potluck dinner served tomorrow after the concert.

"No, I'm fine. You sit and tell me about Mr. Reynolds. Trina says he's quite fine."

Reggie froze. "When did you talk to Trina?"

Her grandmother transferred a large handful of dripping collards from one water-filled portion of the double sink to the other. "This afternoon. She called to confirm my hair appointment for Saturday, and to let me know she was taking Mr. Reynolds over to the school."

"And you didn't call to warn me?"

"Why on earth would I do that?"

"Because you're my grandmother," Reggie said, outdone by this well-meaning but making her crazy conspiracy.

Gram's answering smile resonated from her heart. "I am your grandmother, and I've watched you grow and blossom and get beat down by life and pick yourself up again. Dorothy, it is time for you to put on your ruby slippers and step onto the yellow brick road."

"Great. Now, I'm getting *The Wizard of Oz.*"

"If the ruby slipper fits."

Reggie gently bounced her head on the tablecloth before raising it and asking, "*Et tu,* Gram?"

Her grandmother laughed. "Yes. Me, too." Her next words were serious. "Reggie, sometimes God, the universe, fate, whatever you want to call it, sends us a door that we're supposed to open and walk through."

"And you think that's what Reynolds is?"

She nodded and said, "It's possible."

"I can't afford another scammer."

"True, but can you afford to see where this leads so you don't spend the rest of your life wondering what if? Has he asked you for any money?"

"No. He offered to pay for the demos and the studio time himself."

"Then case closed, at least for me. You get to make the ultimate decision of course, and I can only imagine how hard it must be for you to even think about putting your heart and dreams back out there again."

"No kidding,"

"Even so, it's time for you to gather up Toto and get ready for the Emerald City."

In spite of the silly allusions, Reggie knew her grandmother was right. She was also correct about how hard it was for Reggie to consider resurrecting her dreams. Granted, she'd been younger then, only seventeen, and hadn't known that someone you trusted could rip the heart right out of you. Now, at twenty-seven she was well aware that life could run you over in the street and not care, and she didn't want that to happen to her again.

Gram took a seat at the table and wiped her hands on her apron. "I'll support you either way."

"I know." Gram, whose full name was Crystal Vaughn, was the world's leading cheerleader of her granddaughter's dreams, even when Reggie didn't know she had any. Crystal had also supported the music dreams of her daughter, Brenda, Reggie's mom. But Brenda's had ended on the point of a needle in a fetid room in Copenhagen when Reggie was twelve.

"So, is he really as fine as Trina said?"

Reggie gave her grandmother a look. "You need to quit."

"Come on. Answer the question, girl. Is he?"

"Yes, Gram. The man is fine. Quite fine, in fact." She chose not to mention the sparks that had seemed to flare between them because she was certain nothing would come of them. She and Jamal were from two different worlds.

On the way back to his hotel, Jamal finally thawed out enough to raise his arm and check his watch for the time. He could easily make his flight home, but the challenge of Regina Vaughn made leaving town out of the question. Instead, he put in a call to his assistant, Cheryl, in L.A. She promised to take care of the flight changes and to get an extension on his hotel suite. Always grateful for her sunny disposition and amazing efficiency, he ended the call. Now, he'd be able to plot his next move. But first, he had to buy some gloves.

# Chapter 3

Reggie was whipped from having worked all day, but the moment she walked into the school and saw her kids all dressed up, and their proud parents standing beside them, the weariness melted away. The excitement in the air and in their young faces was contagious.

After stashing her coat and purse in the school's office, she and the principal, Dr. Baldwin, reviewed the night's program. When they were certain they knew how things would flow, Reggie hurried off to the gym to make sure everything was in place. She swept critical eyes over the risers the children would be standing on, the many chairs fanned out around the area for the audience to sit in and the positioning of her piano. Everything appeared to be in place, so she headed down to the music room where the kids and their parents were gathering.

She was wearing her *good* dress; a simple, long-sleeved black dress with a hemline that brushed her ankles. It fit her curves well yet flowed freely enough for her to be comfortable in. On her feet were her black, high-heeled boots, and around her neck, her mother's pearls. It was the dress she also wore to funerals, graduations and sometimes to church. Tonight it was concert attire.

Most of the kids were already in their seats. The others had ten more minutes to show up and she prayed no one would be late.

When Jamal arrived, there were only a few open seats left in the dimly lit gymnasium. He had no idea how many students attended the school but it appeared that families and friends had turned out in full force. He spotted Trina waving at him from across the room. He'd called her earlier to let her know he'd be attending, and she'd promised to save him a seat.

As he made his way, he could feel the eyes. His expensive clothing and bearing pegged him as an outsider, but he shrugged it off and nodded polite greetings to some of the older ladies as he passed by. They smiled back and nudged each other, whispering and giggling.

He took the open seat next to Trina. She introduced him to the woman seated beside him. She was older and sported beautiful gray dreads. "Jamal Reynolds. Reggie's grandmother, Crystal Vaughn."

Jamal paused. Leave it to Trina to catch him off guard. "Hello. Nice to meet you."

"Same here," the woman politely responded.

*Her grandmother.* He remembered Regina referencing her while they were walking home last night. He wondered how much Regina had told her about him. Knowing her, probably nothing.

But the question was set aside as the children filed in and took their places on the risers. Some were dressed in suits and Sunday dresses while others wore jeans and T-shirts.

Ringing applause greeted their arrival. When the smiling Regina entered next, the applause increased in both volume and enthusiasm. Jamal took it as a signal of how much she was appreciated. The sight of her with her hair down and makeup on, and all dressed up in the figure-skimming black dress with jewelry around her neck made him sit up straighter so he could get a better look. The first time he met her, she'd been wearing a shapeless gray housekeeping dress. Yesterday, jeans and a coat and hat that made her look like a brown-skinned Inuit. Tonight, she was hot. Her beauty was on full display and he couldn't decide where to look first. The gleaming shoulder-length hair grabbed his attention as did the soft lines of her shoulders and arms. He found the sultry sweet curves of her breasts and hips captivating, but her mouth, highlighted with a muted toned lipstick, looked ripe enough to eat.

Her grandmother whispered, "She's gorgeous, isn't she?"

"Oh, yes, ma'am," he heard himself reply. Every fiber of his being was focused on Regina in a way he'd never focused on any woman before. Watching her gracefully take her seat on the piano bench, he realized he was rock hard. He shifted his folded coat over his lap to cover the evidence, but never took his eyes off the cause.

For the next hour, the audience in the gymnasium was treated to an outstanding performance. Some of the selections were slow and pure, like "Peace Be Still," while a few songs by Kirk Franklin rocked the house. During the intermission, the school principal, a short brown woman named Dr. Baldwin, came out and made a poignant plea for financial support. She pointed out the lack of books, instruments and even working lightbulbs in the ceiling above their heads. She also spoke of all the academic awards the students had achieved in spite of being taught in a building that on some days seemed to be on the verge of crumbling. Her words were so moving and so passionate Jamal just wanted to know who to write a check

out to. Music was his love and his life. Helping out a place that
nurtured and celebrated that art was a no-brainer. After that
he'd ask Dr. Baldwin how he might help in any other ways.
He also planned to research Madame Sissieretta Jones, the
woman for whom the school was named. He'd never heard of
her, but she was a musical legend he needed to know.

He wanted to know Regina Vaughn, too; not intimately,
although seeing her tonight made that statement a lie. For now,
he chose to focus on knowing who she was inside. She was
tough, intelligent and most of all intriguing, but what made
her tick? Did she have a man? Children? Were her parents
still living? There was so much he didn't know. Watching her
leading the choir in the last selection, he thanked the fates for
bringing him to Detroit.

After the program ended Reggie toured the gym, praising
her students and receiving praise in return from their families
and friends. People were talking, taking pictures and setting
up the table for the potluck. In the midst of the noisy madness,
she took a moment to try to spot her grandmother in the
crowded gym. She saw her over by the buffet table. Trina was
with her and in between them stood Jamal Reynolds. As if
cued, he looked up and into Reggie's eyes. He held her there
as if by magic and she swore she couldn't have moved had she
wanted to. Her grandmother called him a door, but Reggie
had the overwhelming sense that if she turned the knob, there
would be more inside than music. He exuded a maleness that
was as charged as a downed power line and it filled her with
the current. Just looking at him made her warm and *want*.
Mentally shaking herself, she broke the contact. Praying he'd
stay on his side of the gym, she turned her attention back to
the students and parents.

He didn't of course. In fact, when she looked up, he was
walking toward her carrying two food-filled plates. Everybody

in the place was watching. He, however, had eyes only for her, and the depth she read in them made her heart pound.

When he reached her side, she told him, "There are stalking laws in Michigan."

He gave her a muted smile. "Really." He handed her the plate.

She took it and the silverware. "Thought you were taking the red-eye."

"Changed my mind."

In his intense gaze, Reggie saw everything a woman could ever want to see in a man's eyes, and the knowledge that he wasn't hiding it scared her to death. She noticed her grandmother and Trina watching them, too. When her grandmother smiled approvingly and raised a forkful of greens in silent salute, Reggie playfully shook her head and refocused on Jamal. "How about we find a seat."

"Lead the way."

She chose two empty chairs near the risers.

Once they were settled, they started in on their plates. The food was good and Reggie was famished.

"Did you have to work today?"

"I did, and I'm looking at a six o'clock start in the morning."

"Hardworking lady."

"Tell me about it."

"If I want to write a check to help out the school, who should I make it out to?"

"The school. Why are you writing a check?"

"This is a fundraiser right?"

"Well, yeah, but—"

And before she could ask, he said reassuringly, "And I'm not doing it just to impress you."

"You knew I was going to ask that."

"I did."

"Smart and cute. Who'd've ever thought?"

He laughed. She did, too.

"I want to do it because music is my thing, and if I can help a school with kids that love it as much as I do, I'm all over it. I mentor a couple of schools in L.A."

Reggie studied the serious set of his features and responded sincerely, "Thank you."

"You're welcome."

With the current humming in them both, they went back to eating.

An hour later, the food was packed up, the gym cleaned and everyone said their goodbyes. Trina hurried off to meet Brandon, leaving Reggie outside with her grandmother and Jamal. It was 9:00 p.m. and just starting to snow.

Crystal asked, "Mr. Reynolds, would you like to stop by for coffee?"

"Thank you, but I know Regina has to work in the morning."

*Cute, smart and considerate,* Reggie thought to herself. She liked that and so she told him, "You can come, but let's go. It's cold out here." The wind was starting to pick up.

"I had my car drop me off. Let me call the driver."

"By the time he gets here, we could be home."

So once again, the ill-dressed Jamal found himself walking through the frigid Detroit night.

Being California born and raised, snow was something Jamal rarely encountered and it was coming down like cold white rain. The wind blew stinging pellets of the stuff into his face, so he pulled his unbuttoned coat closer and hurried up the steps to the Vaughns' porch.

The wind was howling now. While he waited for Regina to undo all the locks, he shivered as the cold cut through his pants legs as if he was naked.

Blessedly, the interior was warm. Once the doors were locked, he asked still shivering, "Is this weather normal for April?"

"April's never normal," Reggie pointed out. "This is Michigan. Let me take your coat."

He handed it over but he couldn't seem to shake the shivers.

"Welcome to our home, Mr. Reynolds," her grandmother said, handing Reggie her coat, too. "Reg, take him in the living room and park him by the radiator so he can thaw out. I'll get the coffee started."

With a smile, she disappeared into the kitchen.

Jamal followed Reggie into the small living room. By his L.A. standards, the place was tiny. Living room, dining room, kitchen and maybe a small bathroom somewhere in the back. Bedrooms upstairs, he guessed. The furniture was worn but proudly polished. The beautiful framed abstract art hanging on the walls immediately caught his eye. The work, filled with muted reds and blues, was outstanding and he wondered who the artist might be even as he continued to shake from the cold.

"Radiator's there." She pointed at what appeared to be a bunch of pipes resembling an opened accordion.

Puzzled, he studied it. As he moved closer, he could feel heat but wasn't sure how it was being transmitted.

She must have seen the confusion on his face. "You don't know what a radiator is?"

"In California, we don't need things like this."

"Runs off steam. Hold your hands above it like this."

Jamal mimicked her motion. The soft heat that bathed his hands made him groan with relief. "Oh, that's good."

She cracked a smile.

He liked her smile. He also liked the way she looked this evening. The simple black dress flowed around her like a song, giving her a sophistication and a polish that seemed to ramp up her natural beauty. He forced his eyes away from the strand of pearls draped sinuously around her throat because all he could think about was her wearing them while nude in his bed. "I like the paintings. Who's the artist?"

"Gram. She did them as part of her rehab after her stroke. She didn't want them framed, but I thought they were too good to be just tossed out."

"When was the stroke?"

"About fifteen years ago."

"Do you think I could commission her to do one for me?"

She shrugged. "You can ask."

He studied the woman he was developing a craving for. "Are you sure you're okay with me being here tonight? Six is early."

"It is, but I'm okay."

He had no way of knowing if she was telling the truth, but he was glad to have any amount of time with her, even if it was just long enough to drink a cup of coffee. He searched his mind for a topic that would keep her talking to him. "I like your hair down."

"Thanks. Trina does it. Nothing like having your best friend be a hairdresser. What's your best friend do to pay the bills?"

The question caught him off guard. "Hmm. Let's see." He mentally went down the list of people he could call friend, but decided none qualified as best. "Don't have one."

Her face showed confusion. "Everybody has a best friend."

He shrugged. "I don't."

"Why not?"

"Got my music. It's the only friend I need."

"What about family? Brothers, sisters?"

Again he shrugged. "Don't have any of those either, far as I know."

"What?"

"Raised in foster care."

"Ah. Okay. Didn't mean to be so nosy."

"No problem. It's a natural question."

Reggie still felt bad. She'd never known anyone who didn't have family somewhere, even if it was jail. How had that affected him growing up? she wondered. She decided she'd been nosy enough for one night, so she kept the question to herself. She looked at him looking back at her from where he stood by the radiator, and there in the quiet of her grandmother's living room, Jamal Reynolds became more real.

"Coffee's ready," Gram called out.

Jamal's feet had finally thawed, so he gestured for Reggie to go first. "After you."

As she led the way, he watched the siren sway of her dress-covered hips, and all he could do was shake his head and say to himself, *My, my, my.*

Reggie sensed he was checking her out and her inner awareness of him amped up a few more notches. His eyes had been on her all evening; sometimes teasing, sometimes serious, but always there. It wasn't something she was accustomed to. There was also the looming question of whether he was really interested in her or if this was just a game to get her to say yes to his proposal. She didn't like that second part and so reminded herself that she'd only met him a few days ago. She also reminded herself that even though her grandmother had given him her stamp of approval, she knew her grandmother; Crystal Vaughn had a lot more questions. Jamal may have thought this was just a polite invitation to coffee, but he was about to learn why Reggie and Trina had nicknamed her The Grand Inquisitor.

After they took seats at the kitchen table and fixed their coffees to their likings, Reggie, sipping on a mug of decaf tea, sat back and watched.

"Mr. Reynolds, Reggie and Trina say you're a producer. Would I know any of the names you've worked with?" Crystal asked.

He ran down some of the names Reggie had seen on his Web page, and again, it was an impressive list.

Gram looked impressed as well. "Some good folks there."

"I think so."

"How long have you been in the business?"

"Did my first CD when I was seventeen, so about seventeen years."

"You must enjoy it?"

"Almost as much as this coffee."

Her eyes were kind. "Help yourself to more if you like."

"Thanks."

Although he had ceased to be a cardboard cutout to Reggie, the jury was still out. Granted, he was so charming he had her grandmother eating out of his hand, and every time his eyes met Reggie's, she found it hard to breathe, like now, but that didn't change the fact that being a music teacher was the sanest decision to make at this juncture in her life.

Jamal noticed that Reggie hadn't said much, but even as her grandmother continued to quiz him, he was unable to keep his eyes from straying over her mouth, eyes, the sweep of her cheeks and the way she was wearing her hair. That she didn't appear cognizant of how gorgeous she actually was was yet another surprise. So many of the women he met were all about their looks.

Crystal asked, "Do you travel a lot, Mr. Reynolds?"

"Please call me Jamal, and yes, ma'am, I do."

"Must be hard on your wife?"

"No wife."

"Girlfriend?"

"Gram!" Reggie croaked through the tea she'd just swallowed.

Jamal smiled. "It's okay. No special girlfriend either. Ladies don't like being second."

"To what?"

"My music. Can't seem to find one who understands why I'm in the studio 24/7. But maybe one day." His next words were directed at Reggie. "A beautiful woman can move you just like a beautiful song."

Heat spread over Reggie like warm syrup over waffles, leaving her nipples hard and an answering riff between her thighs.

As if he hadn't just set her on fire, he smoothly returned to Crystal, "And I'm not offended by your questions. I'm asking Regina to make a big decision. I figured this was going to be more than just a cup of coffee."

*Cute and smart,* Reggie echoed inwardly again. Her grandmother had the decency to look embarrassed.

"My apologies for being so nosy. But you're right, I want to know all about you."

"I respect that. Have to let you know that I like your abstracts. They're very good."

"I had some health problems a few years back and the painting was therapy. You like them?"

"I do. Very much."

"Then next time I set up my easel, I'll do one for you."

Reggie smiled over her cup. Her grandmother hadn't painted in years. In fact, Reggie was certain Crystal didn't even know where the easel was. *Guess the current is getting to Gram, too.*

"How much longer will you be in the city?" she asked next.

"Not sure."

He moved his attention to Reggie again and what she read there made her feel as if he'd already kissed her; had already brushed his lips over the side of her neck and down her breasts. It was as if they'd been lovers in times past and her body was preening for his remembered touch.

Crystal's even-toned voice broke the pulsating contact. "So tell me where you grew up. What do your parents do?"

Reggie wanted to deflect the questioning before he was forced to explain his past, but he answered smoothly, "As I told Regina earlier, I grew up in foster care. No one adopted me, so I aged out of the system at eighteen."

The impact of his words was evident on her grandmother's face. "I'm so sorry. Please forgive my prying."

"It's okay. Being a foster kid taught me to be independent. I probably wouldn't be who I am today without that experience."

"Jamal, I'm very glad we met."

"Same here," he responded genuinely. "Thanks for having me in your home, and for the coffee."

"You're welcome. There's apple pie in the fridge if you want some."

His eyes lit up with such delight both women laughed.

She said to Reggie, "I'm going to leave you two alone."

"Ms. Vaughn, you're welcome to stay," he assured her. "I've nothing to hide."

"Nope. Heard all I need to. Reggie's a grown woman. She can make her own decisions."

Reggie gave her a nod of thanks. Truthfully, she would prefer her grandmother stay in order to not be alone with him, but she knew that was out. "I'll see you later."

Crystal got to her feet, and Jamal stood, too. His show of chivalry won him more points. "And a gentleman, too? I think I'm in heaven."

She made her exit while an amused Reggie watched her go.

After the departure, silence settled over the kitchen. Reggie glanced his way and found his eyes waiting. Beginning to drown in what she saw there, she cleared her throat and looked elsewhere.

Jamal couldn't believe the strength of his attraction. In order to drag his mind away from wondering if her mouth would taste as sweet as it appeared, he asked, "How about I help you wash up these cups?"

"That isn't necessary. I can handle it."

"You've been putting up with my stalking for the past couple of days, it's the least I can do."

To Reggie the air in the room had become as humid and sultry as a summer day in July. All she could do was acquiesce. "Okay."

After putting on an apron, it took her only a moment to make the dishwater.

He walked over to where she stood at the sink and suggested, "You wash and I'll dry."

"Are you always so helpful?"

"Not usually, but if it'll get me a hearing with you, I'll dry dishes outside in the snow."

His dark gaze was working her overtime, and all kinds of things she'd rather not think about were pulsing inside. "Dish towels are in the drawer over there."

In addition to the cups, the dishes holding the food her grandmother had taken to the potluck also needed to be washed, dried and put away. As they worked, conversation was minimal, but that was okay with Jamal. As he removed the wet dishes from the dish drain and dried them, he was content to watch her—the way she moved, the way she kept shooting little glances over her shoulder at him. He kept reminding himself it was her voice he was after, not the lure of her, or the challenge she presented, or the way she might look nude in his bed and wearing nothing but those pearls now lying in the middle of the table, but it was hard to remember.

With her hands in the soapy water, Reggie washed and then rinsed the big rose-patterned bowl used at the potluck to hold her grandmother's signature jambalaya. She placed it in the dish drain just as he reached to take it out. Their fingers bumped and the sparks flew, startling them both.

"Sorry," they apologized in unison.

A shy smile crossed her face.

"Like your smile," he confessed.

"Yours isn't bad either."

Silence rose while they both rode the opening notes of a prelude only they could hear.

He asked, "When are you going to let me talk to you?"

Reggie got the impression that he was asking about way more than a recording session. She kept her voice nonchalant. "How about now? We're done here." She dried her hands and gestured him back to his seat at the table. "Do you want that pie? More coffee?"

"Yes to both. I'll get myself another cup and you get the pie."

He poured himself some of the still-hot coffee. She cut two slices of the apple pie and placed them gently onto paper plates.

"I'm having just a little piece," she explained. "I don't want to be up all night."

Jamal had been having such a good time, he'd all but forgotten about her having to work in the morning. In his world, if it took all night to consummate a deal, so be it, but this was her world, and there were parameters. He felt the need to apologize. "I'm sorry, and here I am keeping you up, too. Forget the pie, let's have a quick conversation, and we can work out the details by phone or something later."

"I'm good. Have your pie and coffee. As long as I'm in bed by eleven, I'll be okay." She passed him a plate and a fork.

"What time do you usually get up?"

"Around four-thirty, and on the road no later than five-fifteen."

"That's early."

"That's life in hotel housekeeping."

"How long have you worked housekeeping?"

But before she could respond, he groaned pleasurably in response to his first taste of the pie. "This is so damn good."

Pleased by his testimonial, she replied, "Gram's from Louisiana. She can make a cardboard box taste good."

He glanced her way. "You cook, too?"

"Yep, but not as good as she does."

"I'd be big as a Klump if I lived here."

She chuckled. "First time I ever heard it put that way, but to answer your question about working in housekeeping, almost two years."

That gave him pause. He wanted her to sing, not be on her knees scrubbing tubs even if it was good honest work. "Do you like working at the hotel?"

"I do. The guests can get on your nerves sometimes and it's hard work, but it's a job. In this economy, I'm glad to have anything that pays the bills."

He knew she was right of course. The sheer size of his personal wealth insulated him from having to worry about the everyday issues that impacted folks on the opposite end of the economic spectrum, and it made him wonder how the Vaughn women were doing financially. Were they up-to-date on their mortgage or in danger of foreclosure? There was food in the house and they had lights and heat, but were they robbing Peter to pay Paul in order to make their bills? He didn't know them well enough to ask something so personal, nor would he be so disrespectful, but she couldn't be making much money cleaning rooms. Did she have health insurance? "Being in the music business can change your life."

"For better or worse?"

He studied her over his raised cup. "I'd say better."

"I'd say, depends."

"Why?"

"I just do."

"Come on, girl. You can't just throw that statement out there with no explanation. What's up with all this negativity?"

For a moment she didn't respond, but he could see from her unfocused stare that she seemed to be elsewhere. "Talk to me, please?" he asked softly.

Reggie was debating whether to tell him the truth. He'd been so polite and nice all evening she supposed he'd earned it. Maybe when he heard what she had to say, he'd understand the other reason why she was so hesitant to throw caution to the wind. "My mother had one of the best voices in the city. Sang backup for one of the Grady girl groups. A record executive turned her on to heroin and she overdosed one night in Copenhagen."

Jamal's heart turned over. This wasn't even close to what he'd been expecting to hear. "How old were you?"

"Twelve."

"I'm so sorry," he whispered. "My condolences."

"Thanks…"

She looked haunted by her sadness. Seeing it filled him with an urge to make it so she'd never experience such pain again. "I'm not going to rip you off or give you drugs. You have an amazing voice and you could go so far in this business. How's your grandmother feel about my offer?"

"She's all for it, of course. When I told her about meeting you, she called me Dorothy from *The Wizard of Oz,* and said it was time for me to put on my ruby-red slippers and start walking down the yellow brick road."

"I like your grandmother."

"She liked you, too."

"But you don't agree with her?"

"I do, but it's hard to know what's right. I have a job and prospects for a better one if I can keep saving up and finish school."

"Okay, tell you what. I'm going to leave you alone for a few days. I'll fly back to L.A., and then call you to see if you've made a decision." He was not going to let the best voice he'd discovered in nearly a decade slip away. "You still have my card, right?"

She looked embarrassed. "No. I tossed it after you left."

"You're a mess, you know that?"

Holding his humor-filled gaze, Reggie wondered what it might be like to have him in her life for real.

"Do you believe in fate?" he asked her.

She shrugged. "Not really."

"Well, I do and I believe that I was supposed to run into you at the hotel."

"Why?"

"To hear you singing."

She didn't respond.

"The music gods have sent me to show you the way to the mountaintop, and I'm not coming back empty-handed, so know that."

"Now who's a mess?"

He shot her a dazzling smile before glancing down at his watch. "I should get moving so you can go to bed."

Reggie hadn't expected to have such a nice time. "Thanks for understanding where I'm at."

"No problem, but like I said, this ain't over."

She got the sense that he was enjoying the challenge. "If you say so."

"I do." He drained the last of his coffee and took out his phone to call his driver.

Jamal wasn't anxious to end the evening. Watching her, he wanted to sit in her cozy little kitchen with his pie and coffee and talk to her until sunrise. He'd learned a bit more about her tonight, so he supposed he'd have to be content with that.

While he made his call, Reggie checked him out. Instead of the usual black he was wearing gray. On his wrist was an elaborately carved silver bracelet with a huge blue sapphire in its center. The handsome face hadn't changed, though. The thin razor cuts that ran from his jaws down to the well-groomed hair on his chin gave his dark face just a hint of danger. Everything about him was enough to make a woman pant.

When he ended the call and put the phone back in his pocket, she got to her feet. "I'll get your coat."

"Thanks."

More aware of his presence than she'd ever been of any man, she didn't have to turn and look to know that he was following; she could feel his heat. She wondered if he could feel hers.

She suspected he could.

Opening the small closet by the front door, she withdrew his coat, a black wool topper, and handed it over.

He voiced his thanks as he put it on and did up some of the buttons. Once he was done, he stood silently for a moment watching her. That drowning sensation rolled over her again, but this time she didn't look away. "Thanks for not pressuring me. It was nice meeting you." The thought of him leaving for L.A. tomorrow and maybe never seeing him again left her with a strange sense of longing.

"Even nicer meeting you."

A car horn blew outside.

"That's my driver."

She opened the door. Wind-whipped snow could be seen through the frosty panes of the storm door. "Have a safe trip back."

He handed her another one of his cards. "Keep this one, okay? No trashing allowed."

She gave him an embarrassed smile. "Okay."

For a long moment they fed visually on each other, then he leaned down and pressed a soft parting kiss against her forehead. "Stay sweet," he whispered. "I'll be in touch."

Before she could recover, he was gone. Dazed, she closed the door and leaned back against it. Her fingers touched the sweet sting left by his kiss. Her whole body felt warm, opened. If just that brief brush of his lips could deliver such a wallop, she couldn't imagine what kind of fireworks his hands must set off. *Good Lord.* She was so stunned she was still standing that way when her grandmother came down the stairs a few minutes later.

"Are you okay?"

Reggie shook herself free and felt her brain come back to life. "I think so."

"You look a little rocked."

"Does it show?"

Her grandmother chuckled. "He is nice, isn't he?"

"Yes, he is."

"A girl could do worse."

"Yeah, but not a girl like me. He's probably got a harem full of women back home."

"Don't sell yourself short, Cinderella. I saw the way he was watching you at the table. He's interested."

"Yeah, but in what? Probably just wants to put my mop on his wall with the rest of his bedroom trophies."

Her grandmother laughed.

"I'm going to bed," Reggie declared.

"And I'm coming down to watch some TV."

They met at the bottom of the steps and shared a hug.

Crystal whispered, "I love you, baby. Think about what he's offering."

"I love you more. I told him I would and I will. I promise."

The embrace ended.

Reggie gave her grandmother a mock warning. "And don't stay up too late, missy. You need your beauty sleep."

"I'll be up right after the late-night, dirty movie on Skinamax."

A chuckling Reggie climbed the stairs shaking her head.

Sleep was long in coming. Jamal Reynolds filled Reggie's mind. When she finally did drift off, his whispery voice telling her to "stay sweet" was the last thing she remembered.

In the dream, Reggie and Trina were climbing a mountain in a swirling, blinding snowstorm. Trina was above her on the mountain and Reggie knew she'd be left behind if she didn't keep up. They were both perfectly outfitted for the weather, with parkas, backpacks and spiked boots, but the treacherous conditions made the struggling Reggie barely able to see Trina above her in the heavy snow. She kept yelling for Trina to stop so she could catch her breath, but Trina kept getting farther and farther away until the only thing Reggie could make out were the Day-Glo numbers 404 on the back of Trina's pack. Cold and exhausted, Reggie called again, only to have her voice snatched away by the howling, screaming wind, and then she was alone.

Next thing she knew she was in a dark cave illuminated by a fire. Soft jazz could be heard. Jamal was sitting in the corner, and when their eyes met he stood. Dressed in all black, he came toward her. With each step he took, her clothes magically melted away. When he finally reached her side she was nude.

Then the scene changed and they were on a bed and his mouth was slowly worshipping the peaks, hollows and curves of her body. His fiery lips blazed slowly over the base of her throat and the crooning points of her breasts. While he lingered there, his hand played between her legs, doing such magnificent things her hips were rising and she was moaning in the jazz-hushed silence. He was nude, too, now—dark, hard and sleek. "Are you ready to be loved?"

The scandalous pleasure of his lips and hands had her so breathless, she had to fight to find the voice to reply, "Yes…"

So he took her and she came with a long strangled scream, then bolted awake.

Breathing hard, heart racing like a hydroplane on the Detroit River, she wildly looked around in the darkness. She was in her bedroom. Thank goodness! Her nipples were hard. The secret place between her thighs was throbbing and her whole body felt ripe with need. It was as if he'd slipped into her room, made love to her and slipped away again. She fell back onto the mattress. *Mercy!* She dragged her hands across her eyes. One minute she and Trina were climbing a mountain somewhere and then… Every bone-melting detail came back. From the vivid feel of his mouth branding her nipples to the slide of his fingers over her damp core, she relived it all. As his devilishly handsome face shimmered across her mind, she said to herself, *This is not good.* How could a simple kiss on the forehead trigger such an erotic dream, and what was the mountain climbing all about? She had no answers. The lighted dial on her alarm clock showed it to be only two, so she turned over and tried to go back to sleep. Because her body was still riding the echoes of the orgasm she'd had both in and out of the dream, it took even longer this time around.

# Chapter 4

Six inches of snow fell overnight. The beautiful white land-scape was a gorgeous sight to behold unless you had to dig out your car in order to get to work. Reggie's troubled sleep made getting up that morning difficult and Mother Nature's latest betrayal only added to it. According to the calendar, it was mid-April, and instead of the warm spring weather they were supposed to be having, the winter-weary residents of Michigan were shoveling and scraping another heavy dumping of the white stuff. Reggie's car was completely buried, so she was using the blue handle of the kitchen broom to scissor off the piled-high snow hiding her roof, hood and trunk. The temp was in the mid-twenties. The Hawk, as Midwestern residents called the winter wind, was blowing at about fifteen miles an hour, making it feel like below zero on the skin and reducing visibility to zero as well. Even though she'd dressed herself in long johns, jeans, a sweatshirt, coat, hat and gloves, it was cold; the kind where it doesn't matter how many layers you have on, you freeze. And it was still dark.

Working under the pale glow of the light above the driveway and wading through knee-high drifts, it took her a good forty minutes to unearth her ride and there was no guarantee it would start. If it did, she still had to shovel a path down the driveway in order to drive off. She sighed wearily but kept working. On days like this, everybody working inside the city limits would be late for their job because the neighborhood side streets were always plowed last by the city workers, if at all.

Her car started on the third try, and she sent up a gushing thank-you. Leaving it running, she got out, grabbed one of the big snow shovels and began digging her way down the drive. Gram's honey, Mr. Baines, would be over later to clear it completely with his snowblower, but at 4:00 a.m. he was like everyone else who didn't have to go anywhere, still asleep.

She'd managed to clear a half-decent path and was pausing for a moment to catch her breath when she saw a black Land Rover coming up the street. Rovers were built for all kinds of extremes but even it was moving slowly. It stopped at the foot of her snow-filled driveway and a tall man in a nice black coat and hat got out.

"Mornin', ma'am," he called over the wind.

Reggie figured he was lost. "Can I help you?" There were enough of her neighbors outside digging and scraping to keep an eye on him, so she didn't think she was in any danger, but she stayed under the light.

"I'm looking for a Ms. Regina Vaughn."

That got her attention. "Why?"

"I'm here to take her to work."

She thought the wind had garbled his reply because he couldn't have said what she thought she'd heard. "What?"

"I'm here to take her to work. Are you her?"

Now she was really puzzled. "I didn't order a car."

"I was hired by Mr. Jamal Reynolds."

Reggie's mouth fell open.

"Do I have the right address?"

It took her a moment to get her brain back in gear. "Yeah, but if you take me to work, how do I get home?"

"You'll call me and I'll pick you up and bring you back."

"Really?" She couldn't suppress a laugh. What in the world was Jamal thinking? A hired Land Rover? For her? She thought about how long it was going to take her to crawl to work in the snow, how many times she might get stuck on the way there and back, and decided no way was she going to turn this down. "Give me a minute and I'll be right back."

Happy like a kid at Christmas, she turned off the car, went inside, left her grandmother a note explaining why her car would still be sitting in the driveway when she got up, grabbed her purse and hurried back out.

As the driver opened the door he gave her a nod of welcome.

"Thank you," she said, feeling like a queen. She bent down to enter the shadowy interior and heard, "Morning, Ms. Vaughn."

She froze. On the seat sat a smiling Jamal and all she could think about was last night's dream.

"You getting in?" he asked, his eyes filled with muted humor. He was in all black again. The turtleneck and slacks were set off by the thin gold chain around his neck.

Taking in a deep breath, she entered fully and took a seat beside him. The driver closed them in and seconds later the car pulled off.

There was jazz playing softly. The hushed, warm interior reminded her of the cave. The cozy atmosphere was such a contrast to the elements she'd been battling for the past hour, it was as if she had entered another world.

"Got some coffee for you," he informed her. "You take cream and sugar?"

They were separated from the driver by a partition.

"Yes on the cream and lots of sugar. What are you doing here?" Even at predawn, the man was so gorgeous he made her teeth ache.

"Giving you a ride to work."

She stripped her snow-crusted gloves off her semifrozen hands and took the cup of hot coffee he offered. The warmth felt like heaven. She took a small sip. "Needs more sugar."

"You *Cubano?*" he asked, chuckling, but passed her a few more packets.

"I like it sweet."

The driver's voice interrupted them. "It may take us a while to get downtown but it shouldn't be too long."

"Okay," Jamal called back. "Just get us there in one piece."

"Will do."

Very aware of the man in black next to her, Regina looked out of the tinted windows. It was still dark, but the porch lights up and down the streets showed an army of folks in driveways shoveling and scraping their cars. She was glad to be no longer one of them.

"Did you sleep well?" he asked.

Reggie lied, "I did. You?"

"Sort of. I think I'm still on West Coast time."

"How long have you been here?"

"Got in the day before we met."

The tone of his voice slid over her senses and made her remember the question he'd whispered to her last night in the cave, *Are you ready to be loved?*

He looked out the window. "I can't get over all this snow. Does it do this all winter?"

She dragged her mind back to the present. "Anytime between November and sometimes May."

"May?"

"Welcome to the Midwest, Mr. Cali."

"And the city's not shut down?"

"It's only six inches. If we'd gotten hit with a foot, maybe."

"Maybe?"

The coffee was beginning to warm her insides. She had no idea what she'd done to deserve this godsend, but she was thankful. "Why did you do this? Not that you didn't make a girl's day."

"I owed you for keeping you up late last night, and also I hoped it would be a nice surprise."

She studied him over her cup. "It is. Thank you." And it was. She'd never had anyone do anything like this for her before.

"You're welcome." What Jamal didn't tell her was that he wanted to see her one more time before flying home and this was the only way he could think to accomplish it. Once she got to work, she'd be off-limits, and his flight was scheduled to leave before she punched out for the day. "Would you like to fly to Rio with me?"

She chuckled. "What?"

"Rio. I'm flying there tomorrow for a music festival."

"I'm a working girl, remember?"

"I do but thought I'd ask."

"Are you telling me the truth?"

"About me wanting you to come with me?"

"No," she countered, fighting off the heat radiating from his gaze. "Rio? Are you really going there?"

He nodded. "Be there for three days. I have a hotel suite overlooking the Atlantic Ocean. We can walk the beach, take a ride up into the mountains."

His soft voice threw her off balance.

"No," she said with a lot less conviction than she'd planned.

Looking at her as if she were something marvelous and rare, he slowly traced her cheek with his finger. "You'd like Rio. I'll be going to Madrid next month. Have my own jet."

She was melting and her core was trembling. "No jetting to Spain either. Now stop. Put your hands in your pockets."

"Yes, ma'am." Giving her a tempting grin, he slid his hands into his pockets and sat back against the seat.

Reggie didn't know what she was going to do with him. *Cute, smart, considerate, and now, playful and seductive.* Every nerve in her body was singing with electricity. She was destined to lose herself to him; she already knew that. She planned to hold off for as long as she could.

He asked, "Anybody special in your life?"

She wondered when he'd get around to that question. "No."

"Good."

She gave him a look. "Good? Why?"

"Because when you're in the studio day and night, the last thing you'll want to be dealing with is a man resenting your work. Trust me. Very few significant others survive the making of a singer's first CD, and they are definitely gone by the time the second one's in the can."

"Really?"

He nodded and his voice turned serious. "Most don't like having to compete and end up issuing absurd ultimatums about choosing them or the music. Sometimes the relationship wins out, but if a singer is really passionate about being all they can be, the boo almost always winds up on the curb."

"Never thought about that, but since I'm not going to be in the studio…"

"Quit playing, girl."

She grinned and went back to her coffee.

"So, what's your real reason for saying no?"

"I told you last night."

"You did, but I think there's something else going on with you."

"Really? You haven't known me long enough to be able to read my insides."

"A good producer always knows his artists, so spill it. If it's legit, I'll back off."

"Yeah, right."

"How about maybe?"

Reggie looked away from his amused features. Could she really tell him the truth? "You won't laugh?"

"At you, never."

The way he said it made her believe him. "I'm scared," she said flatly.

"Of what?"

"All of it. Everything that could be associated with going into the studio and what might happen after. I was fine when I was younger but now, I'm not a risk taker. That's Trina's job. I stand off to the side and hold her purse."

He smiled.

She shrugged. "It's true. I don't do change well. I like being in my little box with the top taped shut."

"What if there's someone along to hold your hand?"

"You mean like Trina? We take Trina to L.A. we'll never see her again."

"No, like me."

Another heart-stopping moment. She really had no answer to that either.

"And if you think you need a chaperone, we'll take your grandmother. Has she ever been to California?"

"Not that I know of. But what about my job? Who'd stay with the house?" For the next few seconds she ran off a nonstop list of all the reasons why neither of the Vaughn women could leave Detroit, until he finally broke in and said softly, "Gina?"

The intonation and the timbre of his voice stopped her cold. No man had ever called her that before, and definitely not in such a seductive way. "The name's Reggie," she somehow managed to say.

"With me, it's Gina. You're a beautiful sexy woman, not a kid playing third base."

His explanation made her so dizzy she swore she was going to keel over on the seat.

"So," he continued as if the matter concerning her name was settled, "how much vacation time do you have?"

"A week."

"That should be more than enough to do what needs doing."

"But what if I want to use that time for something else?"

"What if your CD goes platinum and you can go back to school?"

Parts of her were screaming *take the offer,* but other parts, the Ms. Practical parts, couldn't believe she was even considering something so life changing without a guaranteed safety net. Dream or no dream.

"Let the world hear that voice, Gina," he implored softly. "It's a gift you're supposed to share."

"Now you're playing the guilt card?" she accused with a hint of humor.

"Whatever it takes," he replied, looking into her eyes. "You're a hard nut to crack."

Reggie took in a deep breath. She drained the last of her coffee and set the empty cup in the holder by her side. She came to a decision. "Okay, I'll do a demo, but I do it here in Detroit."

That froze him. "Why?"

"I'm not risking my job."

"Gina—"

"That's my compromise. Take it or leave it."

He studied the determination in her face. She was serious. "Okay, you win." In reality, Jamal knew he'd won. Once he got her in the studio, he'd pass her demos around. More than a few recording companies were bound to be interested. "Do you have a particular studio in mind?"

"Yes."

"Will it be able to give me the quality I'm after?"

"I think so."

He really wanted to get her in a state-of-the-art sound studio, and hoped the place she had in mind was that. If not, he'd have to settle for fixing any insufficiencies in the demo once he got it back to L.A. "When do you want this to happen?"

"If you're still going to cover the costs, I can do a demo while you're in Rio."

"No, I want to be in the studio with you."

She studied him for a long moment. "Why?"

"Because to get it listened to by the people I'm shooting for, it has to be done in a certain way."

"I suppose that makes sense, so okay."

"Let me do Rio and then I'll fly back here." He stared at her for a long moment.

"What?"

"You're way tougher than you think you are."

She smiled and looked out the window. From what she could see of the outside, they were almost at the hotel. "What time are you flying out?"

"Heading to the airport as soon as I drop you off."

"Oh." It was hard to keep the disappointment out of her voice.

"But I'll call you from Rio. Do you have to work to-morrow?"

"No, I have Sunday off."

"Okay. I'll try not to call you too late."

Reggie knew he was probably wishing she were less cautious, but she was who she was. "I won't apologize for who I am, Jamal."

"I'm not asking you to. I'd just like for you to consider being who you are in a different way. The last thing I want is to force you into being someone you're not. You're pretty special. I don't want to lose that."

The soft response turned her upside down and inside out.

The driver's voice interrupted her reverie. "We're almost there."

Reggie peered through the glass and could just make out the tall signature buildings of the city's downtown complex through the blowing snow. When she turned back to Jamal he was watching her with a familiar silence. She inwardly admitted to being attracted to him in a way she had no business being. "Thanks again for the ride."

"It's been my pleasure."

By then the Land Rover had pulled up in front of the hotel. When the driver stopped, Reggie reluctantly pulled on her hat and gloves and grabbed her purse. She didn't want to leave, and sensed he didn't want her to either, but there was no way around it.

"Take care of yourself," he said.

She nodded.

The door was opened by the driver, but she and Jamal ignored it for the moment. They were too busy staring at each other. He reached over and gently traced her cheek. The intensity made her eyes close.

"Go to work before I kidnap you, Gina."

And at that moment she would have let him. Never in her

wildest dreams had she ever imagined a man like him would walk into her life, let alone make passionate love to her in one. "You take care of yourself, too."

But she didn't leave. His handsome features, the faint notes of his cologne and the heat of his nearness conspired to keep her in place. As they drank each other in with a hunger that was unmistakable, the kiss that came next seemed inevitable. Their slow, unhurried, first taste of each other set them afire.

Jamal would have given everything he owned not to be in the backseat of a Land Rover because his desire for her was sharp and raw. He wanted to be someplace where he could make love to her in a way that slowed time.

Reggie knew this interlude would only hasten her downfall but she didn't care. Every touch of his lips left her rocked and reeling. She slid her hand up to his jaw and gave him measure for measure, only to have him pull her closer and deepen the kiss.

Neither of them cared that the driver was still waiting, or that snow and cold was blowing in through the vehicle's open door. Nothing existed in their world but need.

The driver cleared his throat loudly. "Ahem! Cold out here, folks."

They paused, and reluctantly and slowly ended the kiss.

Jamal traced a worshipping finger over her passion-swollen lips. In response to the powerful moment, he whispered, "Wow."

Breathless, Reggie smiled softly. "Ditto."

He gave her one last lazy kiss, promising, "I'll call you."

Kissing him back, desire colored her voice. "Be safe." She wanted another kiss but before she could succumb again, she scrambled out of the car.

Forcing herself not to look back, she hurried inside. Only then did she turn and watch the big black car take Jamal

Reynolds out of her life. Ignoring the stares and surprised smiles from the staff who'd witnessed her arrival, she left the lobby to change clothes and wondered if this was how Cinderella felt when she had to go home after the ball and be her old self again.

On the flight to Rio, Jamal should have been listening to the new tracks his assistant Cheryl had sent him last night for critiquing, but he was stuck on Regina Vaughn. Her presence was haunting him like the notes of an unfinished song playing over and over again on a loop in his head. The kiss was still resonating. It was good that she'd hustled her little self out of there because there was no telling what might have jumped off. Him jumping her bones, probably. Probably not though. He sensed an innocence in her that made him think a man would have to go slow, and he found that to be refreshing in a world where meeting a person for the first time often led to a night in bed.

The appearance of the male flight attendant broke into his musings. It was time for breakfast in first class, so Jamal took the plate of bacon and scrambled eggs he was handed and placed it on his seat's tray. Still, thoughts of Gina plagued him. *Gina*. Not Reggie. No woman with her looks should be nicknamed after a boy. If her family and friends wanted to continue calling her that, fine. To him, she'd be Gina.

## Chapter 5

Trina missed work Saturday, citing the snow, but she did drop by early Sunday evening to have dinner at the Vaughn house. During the meal, she dropped a bombshell. She was quitting her job and moving to Atlanta.

Reggie was so speechless it took her a few moments to recover enough to ask, "Atlanta? Why?"

"Because one, I'm tired of the cold, and two, my cousin Paula just opened up a new shop down there and she's going to let me have my own chair." Trina came from a long line of beauticians on both sides of her large colorful family. "I can't pass this up, Reg. You know how long I've been wanting to do hair full-time."

She did. "You're just going to pack up and go?"

Trina helped herself to another biscuit. "Yep."

"When?"

"A week from today. I talked to Ms. Harold about it

yesterday morning when I called to tell her I wasn't coming to work."

Reggie was quietly stunned.

Crystal said, "I think that's great, Trina."

"Thanks, Gram."

Reggie asked, "How long have you known you were going?"

"Made up my mind yesterday morning when I couldn't get my car out of the driveway. Went back inside, called Paula and told her to get that chair ready."

"Isn't that kind of sudden?"

"You study long, you study wrong. Speaking of studs." She grinned at the segue. "How'd things go with Mr. Tall, Dark and Yummy?"

Reggie was instantly transported back to the kiss in the Land Rover but kept it to herself. "He wanted me to go to L.A. to do the demo but I talked him into letting me do it here."

Trina's response came from her heart. "You're gonna blow those L.A. folks away, girlfriend. Guaranteed. And when you start making that long money, you can bring me in as your personal stylist."

"Wouldn't that be something?" Reggie asked with a laugh.

"Yes, it would."

Crystal lifted her glass of milk. "To Dorothy!"

They all raised their glasses.

"And to her little dog, too!" Trina called.

The three women laughed loud and long.

Later, Reggie and Trina were in the kitchen doing the dishes when Trina asked, "So, what studio are you going to use?"

"You know who I'm going to call."

"He is the best."

The *he* was Kenny Davidson, arguably the best producer

in the city and Reggie's old high-school boyfriend. "I really thought we'd get married and live happily ever after."

"So did everybody else. Except Margo."

"Yeah," Reggie said tightly.

Reggie, Trina and Margo were the Three Musketeers from middle school until high-school senior year. Reggie and Kenny were a couple during those days, too. The four of them hung out together, went to movies, attended the games, even went to church together. Little did she or Trina know that Margo was the serpent in the garden.

During the summer leading up to their senior year, Margo made Kenny an offer he should've refused but didn't. Margo got pregnant. Kenny's father, Pastor Davidson, married them and the love of Reggie's life became the husband of someone else. She never forgave them.

Trina could see the old pain rise in her best friend's face. "Have you talked to him about the demo, yet?"

"Nope. Maybe I'll just show up. Shock him into a heart attack."

"You show up with Jamal Reynolds, and 911 will be called."

Reggie loved Trina's droll humor. "Haven't seen him in a year or so."

"Saw Margo and the two girls a few weeks back at the grocery store. She spoke. I spoke. I kept it moving. And speaking of moving, I hear you and Jamal were making some serious moves in the backseat of that SUV he took you to work in Saturday morning."

Reggie laughed. "I'm pleading the Fifth. How did you hear about it?"

"Kissing a man in the backseat, with the door wide-open, in front of a glass-fronted hotel? I'm surprised people across the river in Windsor aren't calling in."

Reggie dropped her head.

"And for you, Ms. Modesty 2010, to be necking like somebody on a soap opera? He must have hit you with some kind of power."

"No comment."

"Uh-huh. Hand me that pot so I can dry it and we can get through."

They shared grins in a way they'd done since they were nine years old. There was a lingering air of sadness between them, though, at the idea of Trina moving away; they'd been together almost two decades. What gave them solace was the knowledge that they were joined at the heart, and had been since the day Reggie first walked into Trina's mother's beauty shop and Trina offered her half of her bologna sandwich.

"Gonna miss you, girl," Reggie confessed.

"Me, too. I expect you to visit. Unless you're too busy singing for the president or somebody."

"I'll never be too busy for you."

They shared a tear-filled hug and held each other tightly.

Later, as Reggie prepared for bed, Trina remained on her mind. Having a chair of her own had always been her dream and Reggie was happy for her, but it was hard coming to grips with her best friend moving away. The phone rang. Seeing Jamal's name on the caller ID made her take in a deep breath because her heart was pounding like a jackhammer.

"Hey," she said, hoping she sounded nonchalant. She walked over to the bed and stretched out on top of her old chenille spread. Just the thought of him made her sizzle.

"Hey back," he responded softly. "How are you?"

Reggie thought he had an incredibly sensuous voice. She could listen to him talk all night, making her wonder if this was how people got addicted to phone sex. "Doing good. How's Rio?"

"Not too bad. I didn't wake you, did I?"

"No."

"Did the driver come back to get you yesterday and take you home?"

"No, I called and canceled. One of the hotel's waiters lives a couple of blocks over so I caught a ride home with him. No sense in wasting your money."

"Gina?" He sounded both amused and exasperated. "What am I going to do with you?"

"What?"

"The car was prepaid."

"Oh."

"I have never met a woman who turned down a free ride home after a snowstorm."

"Well, now you have."

"And I'm going to be a better man for it, I think."

She was enjoying talking with him. She'd enjoyed kissing him, too. "Are you having a good time?"

"Be better if you were here."

The softly spoken confession rippled through her blood. "Stop that and just tell me who's on the program."

"Stop what?"

"Tempting me."

"But I like it."

"I can tell."

"I think I'm losing my mind though."

She turned over on her stomach. "Why?"

"Because I'm about to blow off the last two days of this concert and get back on a plane. I have never flown eighteen hours and God knows how many thousands of miles so I can see a woman I just saw yesterday."

She went still. "Jamal, what are you talking about?"

"You, Gina. I'm talking about you."

Before she could react, she heard an announcement being made in Spanish.

"That's my flight. I'll call you when I get to Detroit's airport. Will you have dinner with me?"

Still confused, she said, "Yes."

"Okay, gotta go." And the call ended.

Perplexed, Reggie sat in the silence trying to wrap her mind around what had just occurred. Did he really say he was flying back to see her? She replayed the conversation, and each time the words came back the same. *He's flying back to see me!* Her hands flew to her mouth. She fell back on the bed and kicked her heels on the spread like a joyous child, then sat up and pulled herself together. *Mercy!* She couldn't believe this. More important, what did it mean? She didn't have a clue. She supposed she'd have to wait until she saw him again. Grinning, she turned out the nightstand light and slid beneath the covers. Once again, thoughts of Jamal Reynolds kept sleep from coming right way, but when her eyes finally closed, there was a smile on her face.

Standing in the window of his hotel suite in Windsor, Jamal looked across the black ribbon of the river at the night lights of Detroit's skyline. Twenty-four hours ago, he'd been in Brazil and now he was in Canada waiting for the cause of his abrupt return. *Gina.* Maybe she'd put a spell on him. He knew that was crazy but that was how he felt—crazy. Nothing had ever come between him and his music, ever. He'd gone to Rio to check out a local singer he was interested in working with in the future, but he hadn't stayed at the festival long enough to hear her sing. Brazil had some of the most beautiful women in the world and he hadn't looked at one. He hadn't gorged himself on the fabulous food, hadn't done any sightseeing. Nothing. All he could think about was Gina and seeing her again.

He turned from the window. *Crazy.* He'd known her, what, maybe a week? The longing and need to be with her whipsawing his insides was the stuff songwriters wrote about. No matter where his mind turned, Regina Vaughn was there. Because of his looks and who he was women came easy and often to Jamal, and in his younger days he'd taken full advantage. It quickly got old though. He grew tired of one-night stands with easy women who weren't after anything other than what he or his money could do for them, so he pulled back and concentrated instead on his studio, the music and the people who made it. It was a good life. He was content working day and night, and had no plans to do anything else, until meeting Regina that day in his hotel room. Being around her had turned him from L.A. jaded to L.A. amazed. Her decency, kind spirit and no-nonsense blue-collar work ethic shattered his self-constructed paradigms. Most of the people he knew, given the choice between picking up an unemployment check or cleaning hotel rooms would have taken the check, but she'd chosen the latter and hadn't looked back. To him, she was fresh air and sunlight, and he'd taken an eighteen-hour flight and changed planes four different times just to be near her. *Crazy.*

Reggie was helped out of the town car by the driver. Even though she made her exit smooth and nonchalant, inside her heart was pumping. She was immediately greeted by a woman in a blue pantsuit who carried a walkie-talkie. She introduced herself as Crystal Gonzales, then announced that she was a member of the security team assigned to escort Reggie up to the Premier Suite. That Jamal was waiting for her in the hotel's most lavish suite put a sweet weakness in her knees, but she hid it well. As they made their way to the elevator and stepped inside, Reggie's head was spinning with amazement and her heart was beating fast.

When they exited, Ms. Gonzales knocked on a door.

Moments later, it was opened, and there stood Jamal.

Reggie's knees went weak again. He was so mesmerizing that she barely noticed the smiling Ms. Gonzales's departure. The depth in his eyes obliterated everything. "If you're trying to impress me, you're doing a good job."

"Good to know. Come in."

His voice was like a summer night.

The heat coursing between them would have sent a thermometer into cardiac arrest. She opened the buttons on her gray wool coat. She slowly removed it and let him get his first good look at her in her little black dress.

He smiled.

The soft crepe snugly followed the lines of her body to the knee and showed off her lean, sheer-hosed legs in black suede pumps. The capped sleeves of the dress rode just below the crown of her shoulders, offering the eye a teasing line of brown skin above a neckline cut high enough to be demure but low enough to make a man interested, and he looked all of that. Around her neck, she wore a chain anchored by a simple gold heart, and in her ears the fancy gold hoops Trina had given her for her birthday.

"You are gorgeous."

She thought he was gorgeous, too, in his black cashmere sweater and fine wool pants.

The male in Jamal wondered how quickly he could convince her to bypass dinner and head straight to his bed. Lord knew she looked good enough to eat, and he was ready to get his fill, but the *man* in him wanted to take this slow.

That in mind, he took the coat from her hand and laid it across one of the foyer's brocaded chairs. Tilting her small chin up, he looked down into the face he'd flown across two continents to see. "You're the only woman who's ever made me fly back like this."

"And I suppose you're looking for a reward," she tossed back.

"Any bone will do."

Rising up on her toes, she kissed him, and it was all the incentive he needed to wrap her in his arms and drown.

They fed on each other with a lazy fervor that left them both breathless. He brushed slow heated lips over the warm scented skin of her neck and savored her soft gasps of response. As he blazed a meandering trail back to her lips, he knew that if he didn't make love to her sometime tonight he might explode.

Reggie was losing her mind now, and to a man who obviously knew what he was doing and doing it so well, she was lost—lost in heat, lost in the feel of his hands and lips and lost in a body that was throbbing with drumbeats of desire. She wanted him like no other man before and if this was just a game to him, she didn't care. She'd at least have these memories.

She was so out of touch with reality that it took her a moment to realize he was carrying her. The kisses didn't stop; if anything the intensity increased. Then she was gently deposited in a chair and treated to a few more kisses that made her melt before he pulled away. She had no idea where she was, or even her name. After a few pulsating seconds in the silence, she recovered enough to look around and what she saw spread out before her made her cover her mouth in awe. She was seated at the most elegantly set table she'd ever seen. There were candles and roses, beautiful china, heavy ornate silverware and crystal flutes, all perfectly placed on an expensive, cream-colored damask tablecloth fit for a queen. Her eyes flew to Jamal. "What is all this?"

"I think it's me courting you."

"Courting me? Nobody courts in the twenty-first century."

"Maybe they should."

And as she took in all the beauty, she thought maybe he was right. "I'm speechless."

"Good."

Reggie met his gaze across the candlelit table. First a ride to work in a hired Land Rover and now this. "You're spoiling me." She couldn't even imagine how much all of this must have cost him.

"That's my intent."

"But why?"

He shrugged. "Not sure. I told you I'd lost my mind."

"And I believe you." Maybe she had, as well. All she wanted to do was find a bedroom and spend the rest of the night in it with him. To distract herself, she gazed around and realized they were in the suite's dining room. Above her head hung an ornate chandelier. The table was in front of floor-to-ceiling windows and the heavy drapes were tied back to let in the night. "Jamal, this is crazy."

"I know."

She was truly speechless.

"Look. Men are not known for telling a woman what's going on inside, but you blow me away. I couldn't get back here fast enough."

Reggie studied him in the flickering light and wondered if it was really possible to fall in love in the span of a few days. Logically, she knew that didn't make sense but none of what she felt for him made sense either, and this night certainly wasn't helping.

"I guess what I'm trying to say is, I know we just met and this could be the dumbest thing I've ever done, or the smartest, depending on the outcome, but I want you in my life, Gina. You make me want to write songs singers will be covering thirty years from now—fifty years from now. I'm not asking you to marry me, but can we see if being together fits?"

Now it was Reggie's turn to be blown away and she was unable to hide the wonder she felt inside. "You're serious, aren't you?"

"Yeah, baby. I am."

She was speechless again.

For a long few moments there was only silence.

He asked, "So, yes? No?"

"I'm not being punked, am I?"

"No. I'd never do that to you."

Reggie assessed what she could see of his face and came to a decision. "Yes." As he'd stated earlier, this could be the dumbest or smartest decision she'd ever made, but if he was willing to give it a shot so was she. How often did Prince Charming walk into the life of an everyday girl like herself? "Yes," she repeated.

His smile showed his pleasure. "Good. Shall we eat, or—celebrate?"

The embers of the earlier fire leapt back to life. "I'll take door number two for a thousand, please."


Making love with him turned out to be the most erotically charged experience of Reggie's life.

He played her body like an instrument—strumming, bowing and plucking until her legs parted with wanton invitation and hips rose in greedy need. Reminiscent of the dream, he enjoyed her nipples as if they were his favorite hard candies, and left them damp and hard before moving on. She was twisting and sighing, crooning and dying in response to his wicked mouth and scandalous hands. He prepared her so vividly and so well that by the time he slid his condom-wrapped heat into her core, she came, screaming his name.

His blood on fire, Jamal watched her ride her orgasm and did his best to hold himself in check, but being sheltered so deliciously in her rippling warmth was more than he could bear. She was the sweetest little thing this side of heaven and he had to stroke her or die. Enticing her to join him, he began slowly. Soon, the rising pleasure became so breathtakingly good that he filled his hands with her soft hips and increased his pace. With her purring and rising beneath him so sexily, it didn't take long for his first orgasm to explode. He roared under the force and stroked her until he thought he might die, then slowly collapsed into a harshly breathing heap.

Afraid he was crushing her with his weight, Jamal rolled away. "Goodness, woman."

Reggie felt boneless. "That was very good, Mr. Reynolds. Do you give free refills?"

He laughed. "I can see now that you're going to be a handful."

To his surprise and delight, she reached over and cupped his scrotum with her warm hand. "And so are you."

"Come here," he growled, dragging her over on top of him. He could see her shadow-shrouded smile. "There's a word for women like you."

"Yep." She leaned down and gave him a humid kiss. "The word is *insatiable.*"

His hands began doing marvelous things behind her and the flames rose again.

"Spell it," he groaned in a voice harsh with desire.

Reggie was dissolving under his magic. When he slid a finger into the dampness he'd been toying with so beautifully, she had no idea what he was talking about. "Spell what…" He slid in another finger and she melted.

"Insatiable."

"*I*— Oh," she moaned. His touches took her breath away.

"I, what, baby?"

As he gently stroked her in and out, her body responded languidly to the scandalous rhythm.

"*I—N—S—* Oh, Jamal."

He grinned in the dark. "There's no letter called, oh, Jamal."

His fingers left her. She protested. "There'll be more," he assured her. "Promise…"

He kissed her possessively. With her positioned on top, the twin temptations of her breasts were easily accessed and he helped himself until she groaned.

"You're supposed to be spelling."

In the end, she only got as far as the *A*. Being filled with dark hard splendor was way more satisfying.

When the round ended, they showered. They thought they were spent, but being under the hot spray resulted in yet another passion-filled go-round that left them both panting and wet.

They toweled off and wrapped themselves in the fat white robes provided by the hotel.

Reggie looked over at him and wondered what fairy godmother she had to thank. Kind, generous and a wizard in bed, who could ask for more? "I suppose our food's cold by now."

"Nope. It's warming in the kitchen."

"This place has a kitchen?"

"Along with four bedrooms, servants' quarters, a small movie theater and a baby grand. That's the short list."

"How in the world am I going to be with any other man after this?"

"That's the point. Got you a gift, too."

She shook her head. "You don't have to buy me things."

He eased her back into his arms. "I do, and I will, so get used to it." The kiss silenced any further protests. He took her hand and led her to the kitchen.

The meal was wonderful. Roast chicken, shrimp, veggies, warm rolls. For dessert there were strawberries, chocolate cake and French vanilla ice cream. To top it off, Reggie had her first taste of an imported champagne. It was a night she'd never forget.

He left the table for a moment and when he returned handed her a large square something wrapped in elegant silver foil. After eyeing him quizzically, she opened it and inside there was a large black velvet box. Lifting the lid, her eyes widened. Pearls. "They're beautiful."

"Yes, they are. I saw you had on a strand at the school concert, so I thought I'd get them for you."

They were glorious. She removed them from the box and they were so smooth they felt like balls of silk. She slipped the strand on and he gallantly came over and did up the clasp. The string was long enough for her to wrap them twice around. With one loop sensuously hugging her throat and the other hanging on her chest she turned so he could see.

For Jamal it was a fantasy come true. Almost. But as if she knew him well, she soundlessly eased the robe off her shoulders. He looked down at her brown skin illuminated by the wavering light of the candles and the dimmed glow of the chandelier and rubbed a pearl slowly over her breast. "We're going to wind up back in the bed."

Her nipple tightened in response to the erotic play. "And?" she quipped heatedly.

He drew her to her feet, then brazenly slid the pearls over her skin until her lids slid closed. "Come with me," he invited.

Over the course of the night, they made love in three different bedrooms and Reggie learned that a strand of expensive pearls in the right hands could be quite scandalous indeed. By the time she and Jamal entered the fourth bedroom, the only thing they had the strength for was sleep.

The following morning, breakfast arrived courtesy of room service and a sleepy Reggie poured herself a cup of tea. She had the day off and would probably need the full twenty-four hours to recover from being loved half to death by Jamal. He was seated across the table, watching her over his raised coffee cup and looking pleased. "Thank you for last night, Gina."

"You're welcome," she responded. Just being near him made her want him all over again.

"Do you mind if we take a minute to talk some business?"

"Nope. Shoot," she replied, cutting into her waffle.

"Got an e-mail this morning from the office. One of the major companies is having an open audition next week and I want you to try out."

She stopped. "Where?"

"L.A."

She resumed cutting for a few more silent seconds, and then poured the warmed syrup. "What's the winner get?"

"Recording contract for one CD and the company picks up all costs for studio and recording time."

"Not bad. How long will the audition run?"

"One day. The invite was sent to the top ten producers and agents only. Each of us gets one slot."

"Shouldn't this go to someone who's been waiting longer?"

"Maybe, but I'm going with the best voice and the singer with the most marketing potential, and that's you. I want to get this demo done, then bring you out to L.A. I've a guesthouse you and your grandmother can use."

"Wait, wait, wait. Slow down a minute. I haven't even decided whether to say yes or not and you already have me on the plane and landed."

He studied her for a minute. "Sorry."

They assessed each other and she asked, "And if I say no, what happens with us?"

"I'll be disappointed, I'm not going to lie. But it won't be a deal breaker, not the way I feel."

"Are you sure?"

"Yes."

The honesty reflected on his face and in his voice helped finalize her decision. "Then my answer is…" She paused dramatically.

"Quit playing now."

Her grin showed. "The answer is yes."

"Finally," he replied in mock relief. "Hallelujah!"

## Chapter 6

They spent the rest of the day sequestered in the suite, talking, laughing and making love. From the talking she learned that he played three instruments—piano, sax and clarinet—and that growing up he'd never had a birthday party. That saddened her. He learned that she hated squash, liked old movies and had been captain of her high-school swim team. Through it all, Reggie thanked heaven above for bringing him into her life, and Jamal did the same.

As the evening approached, it became time for her to head home. She had to work in the morning.

"You could call in sick," Jamal said, watching her put her dress back on.

She gave him a rueful smile and used his brush to do her hair. "Don't tempt me."

Jamal didn't want her to leave. He wanted to spend the rest of eternity sheltered there with her, but he knew how much her job meant to her economically and how conscientious she was about showing up. Granted, his ego didn't like playing second chair, but he knew they'd be together tomorrow after her workday ended and he'd have to be content with that.

In the backseat of the hired car, they crossed the border back into Detroit and a short while later were idling in front of her modest home.

"I had a wonderful time," she said to him.

They got out and he walked her up the steps to the porch. They fed on the sight of each other in the hope it would hold them until they could be together again. He traced her lips with a worshipping finger, then kissed her tenderly. "Go on inside before I tell the driver to take us to Mexico."

She let her feelings for him fill her up, then said softly, "Bye, Jamal."

He waited until she undid the locks and disappeared inside before descending the steps again. As the driver drove him away, Jamal was convinced that he was the luckiest man in the world.

Two days later, it was raining when the hired car pulled into the parking lot of Davidson Studios. Jamal checked out the battered old building with its razor wire security fence and glanced over at Reggie skeptically. He'd seen some out-of-the-way studios before but none had been housed in a place with the words *Al's Auto Parts* painted on the bricks outside.

"Don't judge a book by its cover," Reggie told him. "It'll be fine." Or at least she hoped. She'd finally talked to Kenny last night. To say he'd been surprised to hear from her after all this time was an understatement. "By the way, he's an old boyfriend."

Jamal swung his eyes to hers.

"Just so you'll know."

"Thanks for telling me."

She heard the distance in his tone. "This is strictly business. We broke up a long time ago. We've both moved on."

"Why him, then?"

"Because he's the best producer in the Midwest."

Jamal had never been jealous before, but reasoned he was now because he'd never felt this way about any other woman before. "Should be interesting."

"You're not going to trip on me, are you?" she asked softly.

The amused tone underlying the question pricked his ego's balloon. "No, baby. I'm not."

Reggie wasn't sure she believed him, but she hoped he'd conduct himself like the professional all the hype proclaimed him to be.

Under their raised umbrellas, they hurried through the rain and across the cracked concrete lot to the big steel door and, following the instructions Kenny had given her during the call, she pressed the doorbell. A male voice answered from a speaker somewhere. "Yes. May I help you?"

She looked up into the lens of the security camera mounted above their heads. "I'm Reggie Vaughn. Kenny's expecting me."

"Who's that with you?"

Jamal stepped up. "Jamal Reynolds."

For a moment there was silence and she wondered what was going on. Finally, they got a response. "That's *the* Jamal Reynolds!"

Reggie glanced up at the camera. "We know that. Will you open up? It's pouring out here."

"Oh! Yes. Sorry."

Reggie asked into Jamal's amused eyes, "Do you think he went to look for the red carpet, Your Majesty?"

He gave her a soft swat on her butt. "Show some respect."

A beat later, the huge steel door began to rise and they walked inside.

Reggie may have gotten over the dreadlocked Davidson, but from what Jamal could see, K.D., as his employees called him, hadn't done the same. Although it was well hidden, there was a muted longing tinged with regret in the tall man's copper-colored eyes as she made the introductions. Jamal wondered if she knew.

"Do you have a particular song in mind?" Davidson asked them.

Reggie glanced Jamal's way.

"I do." He set his briefcase on a table and withdrew two printed scores. "This is the song the company wants the applicants to put on the demo."

She and Davidson silently reviewed the lyrics and score. As they did, Jamal watched them share a look of what appeared to be shock. "What's wrong?"

"Who wrote this?" Davidson asked.

It was impossible not to hear his accusatory tone. "Maurice Jones."

"No, he didn't," Reggie countered. "This is Kenny's song."

Jamal froze.

She went over to the piano and began to tap out the notes.

As they listened, Davidson stared at the score in his hand. "This is almost a clone of the original. I ended up slowing down the tempo and changing some of these lyrics, but this is my song. I swear it is."

Jamal shook his head. "That's impossible. Jones has been writing for years."

Reggie played the song through and got up from the piano. "It doesn't matter. This is one of the songs Wes Piper left with when he disappeared ten years ago."

Jamal could see the fire in her eyes. "Can you prove it? Do you have a copyright or anything that might back you up?"

"We were teenagers, Jamal."

"That mean no?"

Davidson stared at him tight-lipped for a moment then looked away.

"Then let's get this demo started."

It took Gina only six hours to lay down the tracks. Jamal had been in similar sessions that had taken days and more. In the booth, she applied herself in ways he rarely encountered. She sang the soprano part first and followed it with the alto and tenor. Davidson was such a wizard on the soundboard, Jamal wisely stood back and let him work. Because of their shared past, Davidson knew her in and out. He coaxed notes out of her Jamal didn't even know she had. He handled her gently most of the time, but got on her when it became necessary and she took the criticism well.

At the end, she was exhausted. She had to work the next morning, so Jamal sent her home in the car to get a well-deserved rest while he and Davidson stayed behind to finish mixing the tracks. The stolen song issue silently loomed over them like a dark cloud but they didn't let it keep them from doing what needed to be done, which was to make a demo for Gina that would blow the judges out of their chairs.

At one point during the long night, they took a break. K.D. swiveled his chair around to Jamal and asked, "How long have you and Reggie been together?"

Jamal had nothing to hide. "Not long."

"Be good to her. She was the most precious thing in my life, but I didn't know that until it was too late."

Their eyes met.

"She's tough, funny and rare. Treasure that."

Jamal nodded solemnly and they went back to work.

The demo was done at dawn. Davidson's skills were all Regina had promised Jamal they would be and he was completely satisfied with the finished product. He shook Davidson's hand. "Great working with you. We could use a man with your mad skills out in L.A."

"Thanks, but I'm tied here. I have a wife in school and two daughters."

"If you change your mind, give me a call. Here's my card."

"All I want is credit for that song." But he took the card.

"I know."

They assessed each other and came to the conclusion that they liked what they saw.

"Take care of yourself," Davidson told him. "And remember what I said about Reg."

"I will."

Jamal stopped by Reggie's modest home on his way to the airport. Her grandmother let him in and greeted him with an affectionate hug, which he returned genuinely.

"Is Gina here? Demo's done."

"Very good. She's upstairs. Let me call her."

Jamal would have preferred to go up and see her privately but knew that wouldn't be respectful so he waited for her to come down. Upon seeing him, she gave him a warm smile. Her grandmother went back into the kitchen and they walked into the living room. He took her in his arms first thing and gave the kisses he'd been wanting to savor since her departure from the studio. "Demo's done. I'm on my way to the airport."

"Right now?" she asked, drawing back to look up into his face.

"Soon as I finish kissing you." He noted the tiredness in her eyes. "How about I put you on my payroll so you don't have to work so hard?"

She put a gentle finger against his lips. "You know I'm not going to do that."

"Can't blame a man for trying," he countered. They'd talked yesterday about the details surrounding her trip to L.A. She and her grandmother would fly out on Thursday, the day before the audition, spend the weekend at his guesthouse, and fly back Sunday in time for Gina to report for work Monday morning. Today was Tuesday so they'd be apart only a day.

"I'll miss you," she said.

"I'll miss you, too."

"Jamal, is there anything you can do about Kenny's song?"

"No. Even if I was convinced you two were right, and I have to say I'm not, you don't have any proof."

She didn't like that first part. She'd hoped he'd believed her.

"You're probably going to have to let this go."

"I can't. Even though he and I aren't together anymore, he should get the credit. It's only right. Will this Jones be there when I audition?"

"Not sure. Why?"

"Because I want to get a look at him, see if it's really Piper."

"And if it is?"

She shrugged. "I'll figure it out when the time comes."

"Why am I suddenly scared?" He tried to keep the moment light, but inwardly wondered how far she planned to take this and what impact this might have on their future together.

"Don't be. I won't embarrass you. Promise."

Looking down into the face of the woman he wanted in his life for the rest of his life, he could plainly see her displeasure. In truth, he just wanted this whole stolen song thing to go away. "I'll call you when I get to L.A. And plan on us making love as soon as I see you."

"Be safe."

They shared a parting kiss and he was gone.

Reggie sighed. The logical parts of her knew that Jamal was right. If she and Kenny had no solid proof that the song was his, nothing could be done. But her heart wanted Jamal to have an open mind and to at least consider the possibility that she was telling the truth. That didn't seem to be the case. And for her that was a problem.

## Chapter 7

California looked like Detroit. Seated in the backseat of the limo, Reggie peered out the window at the passing landscape. She'd seen a few palm trees on the edge of the airport property, but the gray asphalt streets, telephone poles and the industrial area they were driving past could have been home. She supposed first-time visitors like herself expected California to be Tupac thumping in the background while movie stars paraded up and down the street with the paparazzi in hot pursuit, but the view for now was just plain old ordinary.

"Reminds me of back home," Gram said while gazing out the window on her side. "Except for the palm trees."

"And no snow."

"Weather's wonderful, though."

And it was. They'd both been struck by the balmy temperature when they walked outside the terminal after retrieving their luggage from baggage claim. The warm weather was almost surreal after leaving the still-chilly Michigan. A member of Jamal's staff had been there to meet them, an older man named Patrick Wilton. Dressed in a sharp, navy-blue suit, he'd taken them to a beautiful, black town car. Once they were all settled, he'd gotten in behind the wheel. According to him, Jamal was presently stuck in the studio but would see them later. Reggie was disappointed but shook it off. Shaking off the idea that the song she was supposed to be singing at the audition was in reality Kenny's was harder to do.

With Mr. Wilton driving what he estimated would be about an hour's drive, she and her grandmother helped themselves to the small buffet of sandwiches, pastries and beverages provided and settled in for the ride.

On the highways, Reggie read signs for Inglewood, Culver City and Santa Monica. She saw more palm trees, lots of strips malls and a handful of Walmarts. Soon however, the scenery changed and she was craning her neck to see out of her grandmother's window as water came into view. A huge, crystal-blue body of water, without a doubt the largest she'd ever seen, revealed itself so spectacularly, both of them were stunned.

"Oh, my goodness," Crystal whispered with awe.

The driver's voice came over the speakers. "Ladies, welcome to the real California. That's the Pacific Ocean on our left and we're driving the famous Pacific Coast Highway."

From her seat on the right side of the car, Reggie could see cliffs and strips of beach and wished they were driving south to north instead of the other way around so she could have an unobstructed view. The road wound back and forth like something out of a car commercial. Mountains and scrubby vegetation led down to dangerous cliffs fronting the ocean, where surf crashed against the shore. The view was spectacular. "Now this is what I'm talking about," she said.

"Amazing," Crystal agreed, eyes glued to the scenery.

Reggie felt as if she'd entered another world. There were

no strip malls or hamburger chains or bus stops, just a grand magnificence that seemed ageless and designed to touch the soul.

Patrick's voice asked, "Beautiful, isn't it?"

"Very," Reggie responded. "Definitely nothing like this in Detroit."

The gray cliffs rose and fell, sometimes hiding the water from sight, only to drop low enough a few feet later to put the vista on display once more.

"I could learn to like this," Crystal said.

And Reggie agreed.

Mr. Wilton added, "Traffic is light this morning, but sometimes there're so many cars out here, it takes two hours to drive what should be a quick forty-five-minute trip. People come from all over the world to take in this view."

Reggie could see why.

He continued, "Some mornings, fog rolls in, and you can't see your hand in front of your face, let alone drive. But then it blows off and the ocean sparkles like God's jewelry box."

Crystal said, "How poetic, Mr. Wilton. You made this retired English teacher's heart skip a beat with that description."

"You taught English?"

"For thirty-eight years."

"I'm a Shakespeare buff."

"Really? Favorite play?"

"Midsummer Night's Dream."

"Poor Bottom."

"Bottom was an ass."

They both fell out laughing.

Reggie grinned and shook her head. She got the joke. The character, a man named Bottom, had been turned into an ass by the magical creature Puck. It was an eye-roller of a joke, but Patrick's wit was a pleasant surprise. Very few men in her grandmother's circle were as well-read as she.

The two of them launched into a discussion of Othello and Reggie raised her hand. Gram said to the driver, "Hold on a moment, Mr. Wilton, the granddaughter has her hand up."

Reggie thanked her with a nod. "Before this discussion gets too deep, I have a question, Mr. Wilton."

She heard his amused voice say, "Shoot."

"Where exactly are we going?"

"Mr. Reynolds's residence is in the Santa Monica mountains near Malibu."

"Malibu? Where all the celebrities live?"

"Yep. Mr. Reynolds is quite a celebrity in his own right, you know."

Reggie knew that, but Malibu!

Crystal and Mr. Wilton went back to their discussion, but the overwhelmed Reggie stared out the window amazed.

Eventually, their car turned off the Pacific Coast Highway and onto a road with a sign that read, Private. No Trespassing. The road was paved, narrow and snaked up and away from the water. A short while later, another turn put them in front of an open pair of large iron gates that reminded her of the intricate ironwork she'd seen in New Orleans during a family reunion many years ago.

There was a guard station and the uniformed man inside stepped out. Reggie watched the guard wave the car through. Mr. Wilton drove on. She and her grandmother shared another impressed look.

Finally, the house came into view. It was a large sprawling brick beauty with a wide circular drive out front. Jamal's home had two stories and the entire top floor was glass. Now she was really blown away.

Mr. Wilton drove past the main house and around a bend to a smaller dwelling made of the same brick and glass. Large cacti stood tall in brightly colored pots on each side of the door. The car stopped and Mr. Wilton hurried around to open their doors.

The air was fresh and sweet with the tang of the ocean. Reggie looked around. The silence echoed over the beds of poppies, tall fat cacti and the rest of the gorgeous setting.

Crystal cracked, "We're not in Kansas anymore, Toto."

Reggie grinned. "No, we are not."

Mr. Wilton appeared amused by their assessment. "This way, ladies. I'll walk you inside, then come back and get your bags."

The outside of the guesthouse may have appeared small in comparison to the main dwelling, but its interior was large enough to hold the entire Vaughn house back home and still have room to spare. The high-ceilinged foyer led to an expansive living area. The kitchen with its stainless steel appliances, granite countertops and gleaming tile floors looked like something off HGTV.

After following Mr. Wilton up the stairs to the second floor, they were given a choice of the rooms. It didn't much matter to them which one they picked. All three rooms were elegantly furnished and had glass walls that offered a breathtaking view of the sky, the hills and the ocean.

Gram turned to Mr. Wilton. "Your boss is going to have to call a SWAT team to get me out of here when it's time to come home."

"I'm sure he'd say stay as long as you wish."

He left to get the bags. They took a moment to explore the bedrooms, adjoining baths and the media room down the hall, and then stepped out onto one of the outdoor balconies connected to each room.

"This is amazing," Reggie said, looking out at the incredible scenery.

"I'm not kidding. I'm not going back to Michigan."

Reggie didn't believe that for a minute. "And never see Mr. Baines again?"

"Who?"

"You are not right."

They shared a laugh but Reggie understood. It was a beautiful setting. The quiet alone was enough to make a girl not want to leave. There was no silence in an urban big city, not even at night, but out here it had a presence she could almost reach out and touch.

Speaking of touch, she'd dreamed about Jamal again last night. They were making love and she was wearing the strand of pearls he'd given her at the hotel. She'd awakened damp, breathless and filled with need. The wanting had been with her all day and she couldn't wait to make the dream a reality.

However, he never showed. He did call later that night as she prepared for sleep in one of the magnificent bedrooms.

"Baby, I'm really sorry. I'm hung up here, mixing these tracks. See why I can't keep a woman?"

She smiled. "It's okay. I understand. Disappointed we're not burning up the sheets, but I'm a music person, too. I do understand. Believe me." She debated bringing up Kenny's song again but decided not to. No sense in ruining the moment with an argument.

"I don't, but it's nice of you to say so."

"If I was angry, you'd know."

"Like K.D.'s song?"

"Yes, so let's talk about something else."

There was silence as the issue of the song hung unspoken between them. Instead they talked about the flight, chitchatted some more and then he said, "I need to get back. I'll see you in the morning."

"Where's the audition being held?"

"Right here."

"Where's that?"

"My studio. It's on the property, so I have no excuse for not showing up."

She grinned. "Exactly." Her tone changed as she said to him sincerely, "Even though I've been kicking and screaming about all this, and Kenny's song, thank you for sponsoring me."

"My pleasure. With the emphasis on the pleasure."

"Go back to work." She laughed. Her unsettled mood vanished in response to his teasing.

"Yes, ma'am. Sleep well, baby."

"See you tomorrow."

She closed her phone and floated off to sleep, refusing to let her worries keep her from getting a good night's rest.

## Chapter 8

The entire world seemed to be encased in fog when Reggie awakened the next morning, but by the time she, Gram and Jamal finished breakfast, the sun had broken through. Gram had accepted Mr. Wilton's invitation to spend the day sightseeing while Reggie was at her audition. After their departure, Reggie looked over at Jamal seated on the other side of the table. His eyes held so much heat she was surprised her clothes hadn't caught fire. "You shouldn't be looking at me that way."

"And what way is that?"

"Like you want to eat me up."

"What if it's the truth?"

Flames of arousal licked at her senses. "I'm supposed to be singing in two hours."

"So? You're not dressed yet."

True. She had on shorts and a short-sleeved top. "Stop tempting me."

He stood and walked over to her chair. He took her hand and wordlessly coaxed her to her feet. Taking her into his arms, he brushed his lips against her neck. "I just want to give you a quick welcome to Malibu."

"Get behind me, devil man." But because she was kissing him back with equal intensity, they both knew she didn't mean it, so he kissed for a few more humid seconds then took her hand and led her away.


The studio where the auditions were to be conducted was just a short golf cart ride to the other side of his sprawling property. When they drove up to the flat-roofed building, Reggie noticed all the gleaming high-end cars parked in the lot out front. She saw girls dressed like strippers going inside followed by men in dark, expensive-looking suits. She wondered if the females were her competition or assistants to the executives. He parked the golf cart and turned it off. "Nervous?" he asked.

Reggie knew she was supposed to be but the echoes of his loving seemed to have masked most of it. "A little bit," she admitted truthfully.

"We can go back for another round if you think it'll help."

She laughed and declared, "I'm getting out." And she did.

Inside, he escorted her to a large conference room. Around the table were the people she'd seen entering earlier. Jamal made the introductions and the suits greeted her with polite warmth. She saw the girls seated off to the side, checking her out with skeptical eyes. She smiled their way but they looked at her as though she were invisible. *Well, now,* she said to herself. The snubs hurt even though she tried to convince herself otherwise.

A few more people arrived; more suits and more half-dressed, heavily made-up women. At 9:00 a.m. sharp, the twenty people walked into the largest sound room Reggie'd ever been in and were asked to take seats.

Reggie did her best to control her rising nerves. She knew she could sing with the best of them, but the other women in their revealing outfits looked more like the singers in the videos. She, on the other hand, was dressed as she'd been the night of the school fundraiser concert, except for the boots. On her feet were a nice pair of black strappy sandals she'd bought on sale earlier in the week that showed off her freshly painted toes.

Jamal stood up and explained how the auditions would go. Each singer would be given one shot. The music would be piped in for them through an earpiece and the record execs would be listening and evaluating stage presence. Reggie took in a deep breath.

The singers drew numbers from a hat. Reggie was number eight. The other women continued to avoid eye contact with her and gave the impression that they didn't consider her to be much of a threat. Ignoring them, she glanced around the room hoping to see the songwriter Jones. So far no one in the room resembled the scumbag thief Wes Piper.

Jamal called the first singer to the mic. His engineers spent a quick second hooking up her earpiece. When the background track came through the room's speaker the girl dressed in stilettos and a skintight, thigh-high purple dress that was way too small began. She was flat, so much so that Jamal politely stopped her before she got a quarter of the way through. He thanked her and told her she could go. She exited in tears.

Reggie's nerves climbed another notch.

The next two were not bad. They were reading the lyrics from the score in their hands though and that surprised her. She'd always memorized the song before going into the studio because that was what she'd learned from watching her late mom record and from working with Kenny.

Both of the singers were well-endowed, however, and their low-cut dresses emphasized that prominence, so Reggie guessed the men in the room didn't mind that they were reading as they sang.

She saw the man posing as Jones enter the room on the tail end of singer number six and she turned her body slightly so he couldn't get a good look at her face. It was Wes Piper. He was balder and fatter, but she'd know those beady eyes anywhere. Anger replaced her nervousness and when it was her turn to sing, she knew what she was going to do and she didn't care if it cost her the contract. Right was right. Gram was owed for the money and Kenny for this stolen song. She walked to the mic stand.

Jamal could see the determination in her eyes and he went still. He smoothly glanced over at Jones and saw the man's alarmed eyes riveted on Gina. Jamal thought he looked as if he'd swallowed a fish. He had paled and he was dragging a handkerchief over his face. When Jamal looked back at Gina, she gave him a frosty smile and all he could think was, *Oh, hell.*

Oh, hell was right. Reggie politely declined the earpiece and as the confused technician stared at her, she announced to the room. "I'm going to do something different and sing this a cappella."

Her words caused a stir and she could see the execs sharing whispers and eyeing her as they did.

"I'm also going to sing this song the way it was originally written before the man you know as the songwriter stole it from the real composer, Kenneth Davidson."

Loud gasps of surprise swept the room, but she ignored them, closed her eyes and began to sing. By the third note the room had gone so still you could have heard a pin drop.

Everyone in attendance stared in awe as her unparalleled voice rose and fell. Although Piper had altered the words and tempo, Reggie sang it as the tender ballad it was written to be; filling it with all of the pathos and loss Kenny had been feeling at the time it was composed. The song centered on lost love and she performed it so movingly and so well because it had been written for her.

When she was done, she looked out over the mesmerized faces in the silent room and into the eyes of the frozen Wes Piper. "Mr. Piper. If it takes the rest of my life, you will pay for stealing my grandmother's money and for stealing this beautiful song."

As angry tears filled her eyes she cursed silently. The last thing she wanted was for him to see her cry, but she was so damn mad she couldn't see. Jamal made a move to come to her side, but she ignored him, picked up her purse and walked out. Apparently all hell had broken out after that because she could hear arguing and shouting, but she kept striding and didn't look back, not even when she heard Jamal calling her name.

Jamal finally excused himself from the arguments and accusations raging in his studio so he could talk to Gina. He found her in her room. Packing. "Where are you going?" His heart was beating so powerfully he thought it might break through his chest.

"Home," she announced, zipping the suitcase closed.

"Gina—"

She held up a hand. "If you could fix my ticket so I can fly home tonight, I'd really appreciate it." Her anger was still raging.

"I'm sorry. I—"

"Not taking apologies right now, Jamal. Just want to go home. I'll pay you back however much it costs to change my flight."

Jamal sensed there'd be no reasoning with her right now. There was a wall between them and she was in no mood to take it down. His heart twisted with the loss. "Okay," he said distantly. "I'll have Cheryl take care of it. Is your grandmother back?"

"Yes. She's almost packed."

"Wilton will give you a ride to LAX."

"Thank you."

"You're welcome."

"I know you wanted me to have this big break, but it's the principle of the thing. Suppose that had been your song Piper was trying to pass off as his, Jamal?"

He remained silent because he knew she was right. He studied her and wondered if he'd ever see her again. "Have a safe flight. I'll be in touch." He gave her one last look and departed.

After Wilton drove them away, Jamal went back into her room, hoping she'd left something behind so he'd have an excuse to call her. Her perfume was still in the quiet air, so he closed his eyes and filled himself with the lingering scent. He missed her already and wanted her back in his arms. Maurice Jones, aka Wes Piper, denied being a thief, but after witnessing Gina's outstanding performance, many in the room had doubts. Jamal was convinced if no one else was, and was pleased to know the man was being threatened with lawsuits if the accusations proved true. He'd even provided Davidson's number to one of the label's lawyers.

But Gina's parting question wouldn't leave him alone. What would he have done had someone lifted one of his songs? *Probably want to hunt them down.* But because it hadn't been his song, he'd blown it off, totally underestimating her strong values and her sense of fair play. Her getting the recording contract was all he'd cared about. Her performance today had been so special that in spite of the drama she might still get a shot, but his single-mindedness had cost him, big-time. Kenny had warned him to treat her like a treasure but he hadn't listened.

He glanced over at the nightstand. On it lay the case belonging to the pearls he'd given her. When he opened it they were stretched out inside in all their luminous beauty. He sighed sadly, closed the box and left the room.

Reggie reported for work Monday morning and received startling news. Because hotel bookings were on the rise again, her job at the concierge desk had been taken out of mothballs and she had been reinstated. It was the best thing that had happened since the weekend began. She hadn't heard from Jamal. As she told Trina on the phone last night, she didn't really expect to.

A few days later, however, he walked through the hotel lobby doors carrying a bouquet of red roses large enough to hide an elephant behind. He looked surprised to see her behind the desk in her dark blue uniform and she was certainly surprised to see him. She'd missed him terribly but hadn't gotten up the nerve to call him because of her angry exit from his home. Not that she took any of it back, but she did wish she'd calmed down enough to let him have his say.

"You got your job back?" he said, drinking her in.

She knew she was grinning like an idiot but she couldn't seem to stop. She was so glad to see him. "I did."

"Think I can have my lady back?"

"Do you want her back?"

"More than I want to breathe."

She melted.

Guests and staff members were staring but she didn't care.

"These are for you," he said, handing her the mountain-sized bouquet.

"Thank you. They're beautiful." She couldn't believe he was actually close enough to touch.

"I also bring greetings from the music gods."

She snorted.

"You have been invited to sign on with the biggest recording label in musicdom."

Her gleeful cry made him smile.

"And Kenny Davidson's name has been added to the lawsuit, filed in L.A. circuit court today, against Mr. Maurice Jones, whose real name by the way is Conrad Doyle."

She stared.

"Apparently some of the record companies were sitting on info that tied him to a few other songwriters and singers he bilked but weren't able to prove it or didn't want to prove it. Luckily your singing convinced a few of the label VPs to reopen the matter."

She just about hit the floor. "So Kenny may get his songs back?"

"More than likely, yes."

She launched herself into his arms and kissed him right there in front of the hotel's smiling manager and everybody else looking on. "Thank you, thank you, thank you."

She placed her head on his chest and realized that in his arms was where she most wanted to be.

"Kenny wrote that song for you, didn't he?"

She looked up and met his eyes. "Yes."

"Thought so."

"Does that bother you?"

He shook his head. "If we ever break up will you have my back like you had his?"

"Forever."

"Will you marry me?"

She laughed. "Probably not this minute, but ask me again in about six months and we'll see."

"Tough lady."

She grinned with her cheek against his strongly beating heart. "I'm just a chick from the east side. You wouldn't want me any other way."

Jamal kissed her and knew she was absolutely right.

# BEATS OF MY HEART
## Elaine Overton

# Chapter 1

*It was time.* Tristan Daniels stood staring out the window of a tenth-grade classroom at Quaker Street High School in Albany, New York, while the thirty-two fifteen-year-olds seated behind him took their final exam of the school year.

*It was time.* He'd known it for several weeks now, but was still unsure how to tell his family. He needed to do this. He *had* to do this, or he would spend the rest of his life wondering... what if.

The alarm clock on his desk rang loudly and he turned to the class. "All right, everyone, pencils down."

His eyes quickly scanned the faces of his students, some beaming in pride, some frowning in concern, others blank of expression. Those were the ones whose minds were already on summer vacation, he thought.

So much of his life had been a dream deferred, shaped by familial commitments. The one time he'd put his foot down and demanded the right to make his own choice, he'd ended up here. Until now, he'd never regretted the decision. But some part of him had always known teaching was a temporary occupation. The music was what haunted him. The music was what called to his soul, and now he must answer it.

He moved between the seats collecting papers, taking a moment to look at each individual student. This would be the last time he saw any of them for quite a while and he knew he would desperately miss them all.

The bell rang, and the room became abuzz with activity as the students scrambled to collect their things and escape the confines of the classroom. Summer break had finally arrived.

"Bye, Mr. Daniels."

"See you later, Mr. Daniels."

"Have a great summer, everyone," he answered, turning his head left and right as the kids he'd spent the past school year with hurried past. "Remember to leave your papers facing down if I have not collected your test yet." Tristan tried to call above the growing cacophony of sounds surrounding him, much of which came from the hallway as the classroom door was thrown open and the kids rushed out.

It seemed only seconds until the door fell closed again and he found himself alone in a quiet room. He continued to collect the tests, thinking about the dinner party he was going to that evening.

His sister, Tracy, was hosting a birthday dinner for her husband, Calvin, and Tristan had decided it was there that he would let his family know his plans. As he continued collecting test papers he let his mind wander, considering how they would react to his news.

He already knew his mother would support him. Katherine Daniels had been encouraging her younger son to pursue a musical career ever since the moment she first noticed his natural talent.

BUSINESS REPLY MAIL
FIRST-CLASS MAIL    PERMIT NO. 717    BUFFALO, NY

POSTAGE WILL BE PAID BY ADDRESSEE

THE READER SERVICE
PO BOX 1867
BUFFALO NY 14240-9952

NO POSTAGE
NECESSARY
IF MAILED
IN THE
UNITED STATES

His father, Ben, would be his usual neutral self, probably saying little one way or the other. Ben had always encouraged his children to be independent, which meant sometimes keeping silent even if he disagreed with their choices.

Tristan sighed heavily, knowing how his sister, older by three years, would take the news. For siblings, they were as different as night and day. Where Tristan was an artistic spirit who typically gave in to his impulses, Tracy was a very no-nonsense kind of person.

She was as devoted to the family business as she was to the family itself and she felt Tristan ought to be, as well. Given that, she'd not hesitated to express the betrayal she felt when Tristan announced his decision to pursue an educational degree and ultimately become a teacher instead of joining her as an executive in their father's public relations company. And she left little doubt about what she thought of a musical career as a way of life. In her opinion, it was *complete* nonsense.

No question, Tristan knew without hesitation who was most likely to give him a hard time about his recent decision. Calvin would of course agree with whatever his wife said. The poor man was too afraid of her to do anything else.

He, too, worked for their father, as the chief financial officer. Although in truth, given the trust fund each were given, none of Ben Daniels's children, spouses or offspring would ever be required to work. But given the strong work ethic they'd been raised with, it was no surprise to anyone that they did.

Tristan was proud of the fact that in the twenty-four years of his life, he'd never taken a single withdrawal from his trust fund. He'd always worked, always supported himself. Of course, his parents had sent him to the best schools and provided for him exceptionally well growing up. But watching his school friends depend on their parents for everything had always struck him as somehow wrong. For Tristan, there was a sense of satisfaction and confidence that came with knowing that he hadn't gotten through life on Daddy's dime, that what he had was the fruit of his own labor. It was important in a way he knew he could never explain to anyone. It just was.

Daniels Productions was one of the oldest black-owned corporations and one of the most successful public-relations firms in the country. Ben was the fourth generation of Daniels men to sit at the head of the firm, and Tracy had every intention of being the first Daniels woman to head the firm. Tristan had no doubts she would do it.

Tristan packed his attaché with the tests from his students and picked up the room, feeling a certain amount of pity for the cleaning crew that was responsible for cleaning up behind two hundred teenagers. He paused in the door to take one last look around the room, making sure he'd collected all his personal items.

His brown eyes closed briefly as he considered the fact that this room and others like it had been his life for the past five years. This was his familiar world, this was what he knew. Now he was about to undertake something that would forever change that.

Tristan wasn't so humble as to not recognize that he was an incredibly gifted musician and vocalist. But how many incredibly gifted musicians had never made it? How many of them had faded into obscurity or lived on the outer fringes of the industry barely scraping by, as everything from backup singers in low-rate commercials to performing on the street? Barely getting by was not an option as far as Tristan was concerned. He would either go all the way or not at all.

As he walked down the hallway past the main office, the principal, Chad Atchison, came out of the office. Tristan stopped, and the two men stood watching each other for several seconds before Chad finally spoke.

"Well…this is it, huh?"

Tristan smiled. "Yep, this is it."

"Sure I can't change your mind?"

He shook his head. "Not this time."

"You know you can always come back. There will always be a job here for you."

"Thank you, but if everything goes well, I won't need it."

Chad looked him in the eyes as if to convey the sincerity of his next words. "If you need anything, anything at all, you know where to find me."

Unable to hold back the emotions, Tristan stepped forward and hugged his godfather. Like Tristan, Chad was a musician. He'd played bass guitar for the former jazz band Montage at the height of their success thirty years ago. The same jazz band that his mother, Katherine, had sung lead for.

The band had had nominal success in its time, but they'd never really had that one big break that seemed to be the difference between legendary groups and those whose names no one remembered. Now, looking at the man who'd been like a favorite uncle for most of his life, Tristan felt guilty for the thought that crossed his mind. He wondered how often Chad ran into former fans.

Maybe in the grocery store or at the car wash. "Hey!" the stranger would say. "You look like that guy who used to sing with that group! What was the name…" the stranger would wonder out loud.

Holding his head up, Chad would quietly answer, "Montage."

"Yeah!" the stranger would say with glee, as the brief memory of a different time in his life would flash through his mind. "Yeah! That's right—Montage. You guys were the jam back in the day!"

*Back in the day,* Tristan thought. And although Tristan loved Chad like a favorite uncle, he had absolutely no intention of ending his life as a high-school principal in a small town while his music became nothing more than the random memory of some stranger he ran into on the street.

But then again, he thought as he continued on down the hall and out the doors of the high school…neither had Chad.

Later that evening, as he sat beside her at the elegantly decorated dinner table in his sister's home, Tristan could feel his mother's eyes on him. They'd always been close, and even as a twenty-four-year-old man, he knew her maternal instincts were alerting her to a change in her son.

He turned to look at her, and she smiled at him. "What are you up to?"

Tristan's eyes widened. "What makes you think I'm up to something?"

She smirked as she tilted her head. "You have that look in your eyes. That I-know-something-you-don't look."

Tristan laughed. "Maybe I do."

Ben Daniels, sitting across from them, had been listening to the conversation. He waited for his son to continue and when Tristan said nothing more, he prompted, "Well?"

"Well, I've made a decision about my music career."

"What music career?" Tracy commented as she passed behind his chair, carrying in a casserole tray.

"That's exactly my point." He glanced at his sister. She was starting already. "Up until now, I haven't really been taking it seriously. I haven't given it the kind of attention it deserves."

"How much attention does it deserve?" Tracy continued, taking a seat beside her husband at the table. "It's a hobby, and quite frankly a waste of your time and energy."

Katherine frowned at her daughter. "I was a professional musician for thirty years, Tracy. Are you saying my life has been a waste of time and energy?"

Tracy nervously glanced at her mother. "Of course not,

Mom. You made a career of it and did very well. I'm talking about Tristan. For years now he's just been playing in all these little local clubs and bars, traveling all the time from city to city and getting nowhere. Not to mention the cost of all that equipment he's constantly buying. I mean, what's the point?"

"I gave you each a trust fund to provide an income and you are free to spend it on what you want," Ben said, as he spilled mixed salad onto his plate. "Does anyone complain about the amount of money you spend on those trendy designer clothes you love so?"

"That's different, Daddy. I need to buy clothes for work. I'm not only an executive, but the daughter of Ben Daniels. I have a reputation and image to uphold." She looked to her right where Calvin sat with his full and complete attention focused on the steaming, bubbling lasagna in the casserole bowl sitting before him.

Realizing he'd missed his prompt, Tracy nudged his shoulder. "Right?"

Calvin looked up at his wife. "Oh, right, absolutely."

Having done his part, he reached for the spatula to begin cutting up the lasagna.

Tristan simply shook his head, wondering if his brother-in-law would ever develop a spine where his overbearing wife was concerned. Deciding probably not, he turned his attention back to his mother.

"I'm moving to New York." Tristan was surprised by how the room exploded in chaos at his five-word announcement. And the person he was certain would be happy for him instead looked troubled.

Tristan blocked out the others and focused on his mother. "What's wrong?"

She forced a smile. "Oh, don't mind me. I had just hoped

you would always remain around here. In Albany, close to your family."

"Just because I'm leaving doesn't mean I won't be back."

She reached over and touched his face. "I know."

Tristan reached over and hugged her. His mother had always encouraged his dream. He knew she would stand solidly behind him.

Continuing to ignore Tracy's ranting, he then turned his attention to his father who now sat solemn faced. "Well, Dad?" he asked.

Realizing Tristan was not listening to her, Tracy decided to reach him through their father. "Please, Daddy," Tracy whined. "Please tell him what a crazy idea this is!"

"Tracy, this is Tristan's life—" Calvin started to say, but his wife's deadly look stopped him in midsentence. Everyone at the table turned to look at the man who almost never spoke out against his wife.

No one was more surprised than Tristan as he sat staring at his brother-in-law in wide-eyed amazement.

"He's my little brother!" Tracy glared at her husband, seeming to have found a new outlet for her rage. "And if I see him making a mess of his life, it's my duty to set him straight!"

Moment of bravery over, Calvin bowed his head and returned his attention to the lasagna.

Ben Daniels stared at his son for several long minutes before he finally nodded. "If this is what you want, son, we'll help you anyway we can."

"You just watch!" Tracy jumped up from her seat and came around the table to stand in front of Tristan. "You are not going to be in town for one week before you're headed home!"

Tracy had never been known as having a calm, rational demeanor, but Tristan couldn't help feeling her anger and hostility was a bit much even for her. "What is your problem, Tracy?" he finally asked.

"I don't have a problem. I just don't want to see you hurt." For the first time, she sounded sympathetic and he believed that maybe his welfare was her only concern.

"I appreciate your concern. But this is something I plan to do whether you like it or not."

"When are you leaving?" Kate Daniels asked.

Tristan turned in his mother's direction and could feel his sister moving away from him as she returned to her seat at the table.

"Next week. I'm taking the train."

Kate took Tristan's hand in hers. "You know, when my best friend betrayed me it was the worst moment of my life. I didn't think I would ever want to sing again. Not only because she'd stolen my song, but because I thought she was my friend. I trusted her, I loved her."

"I know, Mom." And Tristan did. From the time they were little, he and Tracy had heard this story of how their mother's best friend betrayed their mother's friendship and, in Kate's opinion, stolen her only shot at stardom.

Apparently, the two women had grown up together as close as sisters. Both had an interest in entertainment. Monique wanted to be an actress and Kate wanted to sing. As young women they'd moved to the city and shared an apartment. Kate had joined Montage and Monique had begun to take some acting classes with little luck.

Even though they had been best friends all their lives, Kate had not noticed the warning signs that things were changing. The signs that Monique was growing disillusioned by her lack of success in finding an acting job while Montage was doing more and more shows every week in various venues around the city. Since Kate joined the band they had taken off, and most attributed it to the new style of songs they were singing, songs written by Kate.

When their big break came, Kate had to share it with Monique, believing her friend would be nothing but happy for her. She told Monique about the big-time talent scout that was coming to hear them play that night. She told her about the new song she'd written just for the agent, and even sang it for Monique. And Monique had pretended to be happy for her until Kate arrived at the club later that night to see Monique already on the stage *singing her song!*

Kate had been so stunned by the betrayal she found it hard to even stay on her feet and, with her head still reeling, she plopped down in the closest chair she could find. Her fellow band members had a little more reflexive reaction. Chad had tried to forcibly remove Monique from the stage, which brought the club security into the mix. That was when the other band members jumped into the fray, then the partygoers, and before long it was an all-out brawl.

By the time she got home that night, Monique and all her possessions were gone. Although Kate never saw Monique again after that night, the full implication of her betrayal would not be realized until three months later when Kate heard her own song being played over the radio. She later found out that Monique had talked to the agent before her performance and told the man she'd written the song, and although the agent barely escaped the nightclub with his life he was so impressed when Monique later contacted him he signed her right away.

Kate had always considered the night of the bar brawl the night her singing career ended because as word of the fight got around the rumors grew more and more outrageous until no one was willing to book Montage for fear of disaster.

Kate leaned forward and kissed her son on the cheek. "But despite everything that happened, the music is still with me.

Even to this day. It never goes away. I do understand, son. You have to follow your dreams wherever they may lead."

Looking into the eyes he loved so much, Tristan smiled. "I knew you would understand." Tristan also understood that the experiences of that one night had shaped his mother as much as all the success that came before it, and that some part of Kate wanted him to succeed not only for him but for the young songstress whose career died too soon.

He glanced at his father. "Dad?"

Ben simply stared at his son for a moment, then with a single nod of his head gave Tristan the blessing he desperately wanted.

Tracy glanced at each of her parents. "So? That's it? Just like that he's headed to New York to become a full-time musician in a city *full* of professional musicians. Aren't either of you going to say anything about his obligation to the family? To the business?"

Ben frowned at his daughter. "Tristan has never wanted to work for the firm. So why should we expect him to now?"

"I just thought…" Tracy folded her arms across her chest, and pressed her lips together as if fighting back the urge to say something.

Tristan watched his sister's tense body language for a second. "Tracy, the firm is doing just fine without me. It always has." He rested his arms on the table and leaned forward. "Don't you think I get it? The firm is your passion, and you want nothing more than to see it succeed. For some reason, you've always believed it takes both of us to achieve that, but it doesn't. You are doing a wonderful job, Tracy. You don't need me. Now it's time for me to follow *my* passion."

She turned to look at her little brother, her eyes narrowed on his face, and Tristan was surprised by the water that caused them to glisten with unshed tears. "You just watch," she hissed through her teeth. "That town is going to eat you alive."

# Chapter 2

Tristan had never been so afraid in his life as he stared down the barrel of the small pistol. It was nothing like he'd been told, where your life was supposed to flash before your eyes. How could anything flash before your eyes when they were totally focused on the wide, dark cylinder of a handgun?

The young man on the other end of the gun watched him with a hawklike intensity and looked only too eager to pull the trigger. Meanwhile, two other thugs were rummaging through his luggage nearby.

Tristan stood silently, trying not to show fear while he was being held captive in the men's bathroom of Grand Central Terminal. The fourth thug, who was playing lookout at the door, began to make wild gestures.

"Hurry up! Hurry up! Security is headed this way!"

"Just grab everything!" one of the rummaging thugs said to the other as he scooped up two of Tristan's tote bags, now with clothes hanging out the ends. The other thug grabbed up the other two bags while the teen holding the gun on him narrowed his eyes as if he were considering shooting him.

"Come on, man!" The other two thugs were long gone and the lookout was calling to the one holding the gun. "Let's get out of here!"

With that final warning, he disappeared through the door and the one holding the gun continued to stare at Tristan a moment longer before he finally rushed out the door, as well.

It had only been a matter of minutes since Tristan had collected his bags from the train and entered this bathroom but it felt like a lifetime.

He looked down at his hands to see they were still shaking. The young man holding the gun could not have been more than seventeen—maybe eighteen at the most, but the look in his eyes told Tristan he'd killed before and would kill again.

He hadn't seen them, not at all. He'd been so involved in getting his luggage and finding a hotel that he was not paying attention to his surroundings and all four had followed him into the bathroom.

In the back of his mind he wondered what would've happened if security had not been actively patrolling the area. He reached down and touched the side of his loafer where he always kept five hundred bucks for emergencies. The kind of emergencies he'd considered were a lost wallet or being locked out of his home or car, not anything like this.

He took a deep breath to pull himself together and turned to face the mirror. "Welcome to the big city," he told his reflection. And what a way to start. As much as he hated to admit it, Tracy's words seemed to be an omen. *That town is going to eat you alive.*

He looked away from the man in the mirror, feeling more than just a little mortified by the recent events. A thousand questions were racing through his brain. Should he have fought back? Were there even any bullets in the gun? And the most troubling—had he made the right decision in coming here? If he couldn't even hold on to his luggage for more than a few minutes how was he supposed to wind his way through the sharks of the music business? Or should he just get on the next train headed back to Albany? Just as Tracy had predicted.

He closed his eyes and could almost see the gloating expression on her face when he called to tell them what had happened. Not to mention his mother's worried concern. He knew she would plead with him to come home at once.

He would deal with all that later; right now he just needed to get his credit cards canceled. He started to pull out his cell phone to call for help and then remembered, the thieves had gotten that, too.

He opened the door and saw the security guard who'd made his attackers nervous leaning against a baluster a few feet away. He glanced around, but as expected the thieves were long gone. He headed toward the guard, deciding that the only way forward was to deal with the things he could and worry about the rest later.

Three nights later, Tristan was standing at the window of the budget hotel where he'd taken a room using part of his emergency money. He was biding his time, waiting for his credit cards to be replaced as well as his cell phone.

The smart thing, of course, would've been to find the nearest bank and take a withdrawal from his trust fund to hold him over. Right now, he could be resting up in some plush five-star Manhattan hotel. But to his way of thinking, that would've been surrendering, and he wasn't yet ready to surrender. No, he would find a paying gig and live off what he made, just as he'd always done.

In the end, he'd decided not to tell his family what had happened. But more important, he'd also decided he would not let anything, not even the memory of a pistol in his face, stop him from pursuing his dream. He'd come to New York for his music and he would not leave without giving his music a chance.

He picked up the newspaper section he'd laid on a nearby table and scanned it quickly, as if expecting something new to magically appear. He'd already read through the entire classified section, circling every ad for guitarist, surprised to find there were so many. But still something was holding him back, something keeping him from actually leaving the hotel room. It wasn't fear, he was certain of that. Was it self-doubt?

The past three days had given Tristan time to reflect on life in a way he never had before. He was almost twenty-five years old, and for the most part had led a charmed life. His parents' wealth and social standing had gone far in shielding him from the harsh disappointments of life.

As the only male and youngest child of Kate and Ben Daniels, the world had always been presented as one big opportunity for Tristan. As a child, he'd never been denied a single material desire. And yet, the values he'd been taught along with that excessive indulgence had somehow created a well-balanced, well-adjusted human being, instead of a self-centered jerk.

He'd grown up in the bosom of a close-knit family. Raised by loving parents who instead of demanding he fall into line and go into the family business had encouraged him to dream and to pursue those dreams wherever they led. Of course, there was some disappointment that he had not fallen in love with the firm in the way Tracy had, but despite that they'd never been anything but supportive.

He had a great job as a teacher, but it was obviously no coincidence that his first teaching job had been offered to him by a friend of his mother. And now he was left to wonder how much of that had been through his own work and talent and how much had been gifted by family and friends.

In Albany, Tristan had lived in his own apartment, paid his own bills and led his own life. But it had all been done with the knowledge that the loving cushion of his family was there to catch him if he fell.

Now, for the first time in his life, he was flying without a net. Whatever happened here would be by his own hand. The realization was both scary and invigorating, and despite the rocky start he was determined to make the most of it.

He was a gifted musician, but he didn't fool himself into thinking that success and stardom would just fall into his lap. He would have to prove himself.

He tossed the newspaper to the side and picked up his guitar, stringing the first song that came to mind. It was a song he'd written for his high-school girlfriend, Trisha.

It had been the first time he'd tried his hand at a love song, and as he played the chords he realized the music still moved him long after his passion for Trisha had frizzled out. Music was his eternal love. It had always been and it would always be.

As he strummed the soft melody, he realized that even after all his soul-searching and agonizing over the decision to come to New York, it had been inevitable. The music would've guided him here eventually. And now that he was here, the music would find a way to guide him forward. He just simply had to trust the music.

Something in the paper caught his eye. He stopped playing and picked up the paper to read an ad he'd missed earlier. A bass guitarist ad for a club called Optimus. Taking out his pen, he circled the ad and then returned to his music.

# Chapter 3

Tristan entered the club and, because it was particularly dim inside compared to the bright light of the midday sun, it felt as if he was suddenly plunged into darkness.

He took a moment to let his eyes adjust, then glanced around the club. Even in the low light he could see why Optimus was one of the hot spots. Everything about the place oozed elegance and a style different from anything he'd ever seen before.

Instead of the typical open-floor format of seating, the large room was divided into equally sized alcoves, each separated by sheer white panels that hung casually from corner to corner.

In each alcove was a large, half-circular leather sofa complete with pillows and black barstools for drinks and snacks. Despite its ultramodern appearance, the whole scene instantly brought to mind something he'd seen in a book describing a Roman emperor's palace.

The recessed lighting cast a purple haze over the entire

area and highlighted the black marble dance floor. Opposite the entrance was a large elevated stage, larger than any he'd ever played on. But trying to compare some of the dives he'd worked in Albany to this place would've been a futile exercise. This was the big-time.

"Can I help you?" A soft female voice came from somewhere in the back corner where the well-lit bar sat taking up most of one wall.

"I'm here to audition for the bass player opening."

A melodic chuckle floated on the air and Tristan was instantly captivated. He moved toward the sound but could see no one, just the empty bar.

"That's funny to you?" he asked the voice, his eyes still searching the room.

"No. I apologize. I'm sure you're probably very talented, we're just looking for someone with more...*experience*."

He stopped in the middle of the room. "So, I'm being dismissed without so much as an audition?" He turned in a circle, his eyes combing every inch of the place, determined to find the owner of the sultry voice.

"Did I bruise your ego?" she asked. Tristan realized he was now more fixated on the smoky voice than he was the audition.

"A little."

"Sorry, I didn't mean to. You can audition—if you like."

"Would it make a difference?"

"No. But you might feel better."

"You coming out of the shadows would make me feel better."

"Now why would I do that? Here I have the advantage."

In that moment, Tristan determined that there was no way he was leaving the place until he'd met the woman that went with that voice. Whether or not he got the gig wasn't even an issue anymore.

He started toward the bar again, and was slightly dumb-founded that he could clearly decipher that the voice was coming from that area but there was no one there.

"So?" she asked. "Do you want to audition?"

"No, but I want to meet you. Stop hiding—what are you afraid of?"

"There is very little I fear," she said. "And certainly not some pretty-boy bass player." The throaty sound seemed to be affecting the man in him the way nothing had in a long time.

He shook his head. "Name-calling already? We just met."

She laughed again. "Go away, pretty boy, I have work to do."

"What if I said I wanted that audition after all?"

"Too late, that offer was made five minutes ago when I was still concerned with your bruised ego. Goodbye."

"Wait!"

The room was quiet for so long, Tristan was certain she had disappeared. His overactive imagination immediately began to conjure images, weaving beautiful fantasies out of thin air. He felt as if he'd been bested by a mischievous fairy.

Then she released a heavy sigh and Tristan felt such a relief pour through his whole being it startled him.

"What now, pretty boy?"

Tristan searched his mind for the perfect words, some-thing—anything that would captivate her as she'd captivated him. Having nothing better to offer, he instinctively began to sing.

Like a siren's call, Rayne Phillips felt herself being un-controllably pulled out of the shadows and toward the handsome young man.

Unknowingly, he'd stopped in just the spot on the dance floor where the lights and shadows met, and the effect created the illusion of a halo around his head. Rayne, being a believer in signs, took the false halo as an omen. There was something special about this man. She'd known it the moment he entered the club.

*His voice.* She'd been around music and musicians all her life, but she'd never heard anything like the soothing, mellow tenor of his voice.

As best her mind could describe it was some kind of perfect blending of the soulful sound of Sam Cooke and Luther Vandross's velvety smoothness.

Where had he come from? she wondered. And why would anyone—with that voice—be looking for a job as a bass player in a small club?

Rayne had been on her way to the bar to collect the previous night's receipts when she saw him enter the club. At first she assumed it was the mailman, until the man moved farther into the room and she realized the thing slung over his shoulder was not a mailbag but a guitar.

Her eyes were immediately drawn to his masculine beauty as he surveyed her club. He was gorgeous, she thought. Rich, dark-chocolate skin covered refined features. Almond-shaped eyes, a sharp nose and lush lips. But she'd known her fair share of gorgeous men, and she'd learned the hard way that a pretty face told you little about the hearts of men.

No, it wasn't his face that had caused her to pause in the shadows. It was his aura. That indefinable something that every person possessed. His was radiating such warmth she felt it across the room.

As he stood taking in the decor of the club, she followed his eyes, feeling a certain pride as she watched the expressions on his face change from interest to impressed. She knew her club was one of the best in the city. She'd worked hard to make it so.

And just as she'd built her nightclub from a joint only the

locals knew about to a national name, she was determined to do so with the band she managed.

Optimus Four was made up of four extremely talented men. But there was something missing, something that was keeping them from breaking out of the box of small-time club band. Rayne had known this for some time. She just didn't know what that something was…until the man before her began to sing.

Moving across the room, the minute her face felt the bright track lighting that surrounded the bar, the beautiful sound stopped. He'd achieved his goal. He'd coaxed her out into the light.

Tristan felt his breath catch in his throat. He wasn't sure exactly what he'd expected but it wasn't the woman who was walking toward him. For a moment, he wondered if his active imagination had gone too far and actually formed his perfect fantasy. Because this woman was beyond anything that could be described by so tame a word as *pretty,* or even the overly used *beautiful*. No, she was stunning—absolutely stunning.

As ridiculous as the thought was, the first image that came to mind was some kind of comic book superheroine. She had that kind of larger-than-life look to her. Everything from her copper-brown skin to the multihued hair that resembled a lion's mane, all gold and brown with flecks of burnished orange. Combed away from her perfect oval-shaped face, the thick stuff fell in loose ringlets down her back to her waist. She was very slender and tall. In fact, Tristan realized with some discomfort, she was slightly taller than his own five-foot-eleven frame.

She wore a sleeveless, formfitting black dress than touched every curve of her slender body before stopping short just above her knees. A thin gold chain belt hung loosely around her body and settled comfortably low on her hips. The gold dragon charm than dangled from the belt at the apex of her body drew the eye.

Tristan's ego was appeased when he took in the four-inch black patent leather stiletto go-go boots that covered the fishnet stockings and the copper skin beneath them.

Her long brown arms were bare except for a gold dragon armlet on her upper right arm. Noticing a pattern, his eyes were drawn up to her ears. Just as he expected, twin gold dragons dangled there twinkling as the light bounced off them. But she wore no other jewelry, no chains around her neck or rings decorating her fingers.

She came to a stop directly in front of him, and he subconsciously took in a deep breath of her soft perfume. Entranced by everything from her smoky voice to her exotic appearance, Tristan could not stop the victorious smile that spread across his face. "Well…hello there."

He watched as she reluctantly returned the smile, and although he was certain they'd never met, Tristan felt something was strangely familiar about the woman.

"Maybe experience is not so important." She shrugged. "Okay, you're hired."

He frowned. "But you haven't even heard me play."

"I've heard enough." She extended her hand. "Rayne Phillips. And you are?"

"Tristan, Tristan Daniels. Nice to meet you, Rayne Phillips." He glanced around the club. "Since you're doing the hiring and firing, I assume you're the manager?"

She arched a perfectly groomed sandy-brown eyebrow at him and placed her right hand on her hip. "You know what they say about assumptions."

His eyes roamed over her long body with blatant interest. "I can't seem to recall exactly." He walked slightly to her left, angling his body to see around her. "I think it had something to do with asses."

"You sure you want this job?"

He laughed. "Sorry, sorry." He straightened his body and looked her directly in the eyes. "So, what now?"

"Now we fill out the paperwork to make it legal." She turned and headed back toward the shadowed area she'd come from and gestured for Tristan to follow, which he was more than happy to do. "The guys will be here soon and I'll make the introductions."

Once they rounded the end of the bar Tristan saw the open hallway leading to the back of the club. Because of the lighting, the wide opening was completely shielded by the bar. He realized from that vantage point she had probably seen him from the moment he had entered the club.

"The guys?" he asked, enjoying the view as he kept pace a few steps behind her.

"You'll be the fifth member of my in-house band, Optimus Four." She glanced at him over her shoulder. "As of tonight, it will be Optimus Five."

Halfway down the hall she went through a door on the left and Tristan followed her into the office. One look at the pictures on the walls and Tristan immediately realized his mistake.

One whole wall was dedicated to pictures of the club's evolution, from start to finish, the signing of the lease, to the painting of the walls, right down to the installation of the furniture. Rayne was in almost every one of those pictures.

"You're the owner," he said, in a matter-of-fact tone.

"Yes, I am. Have a seat." She leaned against the front of the large desk and gestured to the oversize red chairs in front of it. "Before we go any further, I have a few questions I'd like to ask you."

"Such as?" Seeing she was all business now, Tristan pulled his guitar strap over his head and sat it next to the chair before taking a seat. He assured himself there would be time later to get to know each other better. And he had every intention of getting to know Rayne Phillips better.

"Well, first of all, where did you learn to sing like that? Have you had any professional training? And why are you working as a guitarist when you have the vocals of an angel?"

Tristan's eyes widened in surprise at the compliment. "Um...thanks. I wouldn't say vocals of an angel, but—"

Her mouth twisted in an annoyed expression. "Look, I have a low tolerance for bull, you should know that up front. You have a gift. Lucky for you, it's a marketable gift. So, stop the false modesty and let's just be real with each other. Why are you playing bass when you could be leading a band straight onto a record label? Have you ever recorded?"

Tristan stared into her brown eyes for several seconds before he sighed inwardly, wondering how much to say. What would a world-savvy woman like Rayne Phillips think of the simple little life he'd led in Albany? Full-time schoolteacher, part-time musician. Not that he was ashamed of his life, but he wanted a chance to get to know this woman, and he knew instinctively she would never waste her time with what she perceived as a country bumpkin. And, unfortunately, his limited experiences put him firmly in the bumpkin category.

"Okay, truth of the matter is that up until three weeks ago I was teaching English to tenth graders."

"Seriously?"

"And the closest I've ever gotten to a record label is the music section at Borders."

He watched as her lovely head tilted to one side and then the other. "I don't understand."

"I've only been in New York a few days. I quit my teaching job to move here. I decided it's time to get serious about my music."

"So, you've had no professional training whatsoever?"

"I wouldn't say that. My mother is a retired jazz singer. She's trained me from the time I could walk."

She smiled, and Tristan felt it as if she'd touched him. "She did an excellent job. Your vocal range is impressive to say the least." She folded her arms across her chest. "Let me get right to the point. In addition to running Optimus, I *manage* the Optimus Four. They are a really good band but we need a lead singer. Tristan, I want you to be that singer."

Tristan's eyes widened again, stunned by the speed with which things were moving. "Whoa. Um…not to seem ungrateful, but you're offering this to me just based on what you heard out there?" He gestured over his shoulder.

"Yes, I am. It's providence. We've been looking for someone like you for quite some time, so why not?" She stood and walked around the desk. "First, I need you to fill out these tax forms."

Tristan shook his head, feeling as if he was walking in some kind of daze as she set the papers on the desk in front of him. As he completed the forms, Rayne sat quietly behind the desk.

Tristan tried hard to keep his mind on what she was offering and off the woman herself, but that was damn near impossible with her perfume filling the air. "Are you a musician?" he finally asked as he filled out the application.

"Me? No."

He continued to write with his head down, but he couldn't shake the feeling that Rayne was in show business. She seemed to be an expert at making herself the most interesting aspect of any room. Or at least she was to him.

He glanced up at her and was struck again by that feeling of déjà vu. "I know we've never met before, but you look so familiar."

Her light brown eyes darted to his and then quickly away. "I guess I have that kind of common face."

"No, there is nothing common about you." Tristan shook his head slowly, as he watched her caramel skin darken slightly with a blush.

"How old are you?" She sighed.

"Excuse me?"

"I did commercials as a child. If you're in the right age group, you've probably seen—"

"The Okey-Oaks Cereal girl! I remember you!"

She gave an embarrassed shrug, which looked strangely out of place on such a confident woman. "That's my claim to fame."

He laughed. "Man—I had a mad crush on you!"

She opened her mouth to respond but just then they both heard noises and voices coming through the office door. "That is probably the guys." She stood. "Can you excuse me for a moment while I go let them know you're here?"

She walked out of the room, her black skirt clinging to all the most interesting parts, moving with the sinuous shifting of her body.

As the door closed, Tristan shook his head in stunned amazement. "The Okey-Oaks girl." He laughed to himself, remembering the little ponytailed girl in those commercials. The Okey-Oaks girl had been a few years older than Tristan, which meant that Rayne was in her late twenties.

Now, she was all grown up and running her own nightclub. And he was the new lead singer of her in-house band. He shook his head again, thinking how differently the day was turning out than what he'd expected. He'd fully expected to spend the day going from club to club and hoping to get a couple of on-the-spot auditions. Instead he'd just got a job working for one of the most interesting women he'd ever met. He returned his attention to filling out the paperwork. Apparently, the charmed life lived on.

Down the hall, Rayne knocked on the dressing-room door of the band.

"Come on in, Rayne," a masculine voice called.

"Hey, guys." She entered the room, closing the door behind her. Four men were positioned around the room as they prepared for rehearsal. Ronnie, Dex, Steve and Toby, the men who made up Optimus Four, all turned when they heard her enter.

"What's up, Rayne?" Dex, the drummer, was rummaging through the closet. "You look like you're about to burst."

"I found him! Or better yet, he found us."

"Who?" Ronnie, the keyboard player, asked.

"Our new lead singer. He's in the other room filling out employment forms right now."

"Wait a minute." Steve, the guitarist, was leaning back in his chair, but he sat up straight at the announcement. "I thought we said we would do the auditions together."

Rayne held up her hands. "Actually, he didn't come about the lead singer job, he came about the guitarist opening. But, Steve, wait until you hear him. I'm telling you, he's the one."

The men all exchanged worried looks. "So, you just signed him. Just like that?" Toby, the other keyboard player, asked.

"No, I've *employed* him. But we haven't signed a contract. I would never do that without talking to you guys first. Just hear him, okay?" She looked at each man. "Look, Mel told me that as soon as we could get a lead singer, he would be interested in hearing what we can do." She paused to let that sink in. "This is the opportunity we've all been waiting for. Trust me, this guy is incredible. Just hear him—for me."

Slowly heads nodded in agreement and Rayne let herself out of the room. She stood in the hall for several seconds thinking of the last time she'd talked to her ex-boyfriend, music producer Melvin Ferrell. She'd invited him to the club to hear the group on several occasions but Mel had made it perfectly clear that his label was only interested in traditional groups, which included a lead singer. Up until now, Steve had been filling that role and he had a good voice. But he was a much better guitarist than he was a singer.

Just in that little bit she'd heard, Rayne knew Tristan was a rare talent and she had every intention of snatching him up before anyone else did. She meant what she said—she would never sign him without the guys' approval. They were a team, after all. But she would do anything and everything to make sure the guys realized how special Tristan was.

She opened her office door and was struck again by his good looks, wondering how such a perfect lead singer had fallen right into her lap. "Ready?"

He stood, picked up his guitar and followed her back down the hall where she opened the dressing-room door and the five men came face-to-face.

"Everyone, this is Tristan Daniels." She gestured to the group. "Tristan, this is Dex, our drummer, Toby and Ronnie on keyboards and Steve our guitarist." She slowly backed out the door. "I'm going to give you guys some time to get to know each other. Be back in a little while." And the door closed.

The moment the door closed, Tristan found himself instantly on guard. The other four men sat watching him with wary expressions and the room was completely quiet.

The hairs on the back of his neck stood up at the realization that every man in this room had known Rayne longer than he had. That thought, unfortunately, led to the idea that one of them could even be dating her now.

"So…" Dex's slow drawl broke the strained silence. "When do we get to hear these golden lungs of yours?"

"Golden lungs?" Tristan asked, turning to face the older man.

"According to Rayne," Toby piped in from behind him, "you're the one."

"So, let's hear it." Steve stood, folding his arms across his chest.

Tristan instinctively wanted to tell them all where to put their pop quiz, but then again, when would he get another opportunity like this? And after the week he'd had, he needed all the breaks he could get.

"What do you want to hear?" He pulled his bass from the case.

"Marvin Gaye," Dex called out. "Give us a little bit of 'What's Going On.'"

"Naw, man." Steve smiled. "That's too easy. How about… Etta James, 'At Last.'"

Tristan quietly tuned his bass while the four men burst into laughter. Once again he considered just leaving.

Then Toby surprised him. He quickly glanced at the others before saying, "How about…Luther's 'Give Me the Reason.'"

Tristan shrugged dismissively and began to play before anyone could suggest something else. The room was completely silent while he performed and once he was finished, he had to look around to be sure he was not alone. All four men sat watching him with something akin to surprise on their faces.

Finally Steve said, "Wow, man. I've never heard it sung like that."

Dex nodded in agreement. "I owe you an apology, brother. That was hot."

Toby just nodded his agreement, still staring at Tristan in surprise.

Steve stood and clapped his hands with a wide grin. "Well, fellas, let's get this rehearsal under way."

# Chapter 4

It was almost a week before Rayne discovered his living arrangements. It was around four in the morning and everyone had already left. Tristan had made a habit of waiting for Rayne every night, surprised that everyone who worked for her would simply leave her to lock up alone in the middle of the night.

As they left the club it was pouring rain, so Tristan pulled his coat up around his shoulders and headed down the avenue toward the hotel as he did every night. But this night Rayne called out to stop him.

"Wanna share a cab?"

He smiled and shrugged. "No, thanks."

"It's coming down like crazy. You're gonna catch pneumonia." She walked toward him until her umbrella was covering both of them.

She smiled. "And we can't have you getting sick, can we? The word's getting around about you. The club has been more full these past few nights than it's been in a while."

Tristan tried to ignore the way the water dripping off the edge of the umbrella fell on her face and lips. She was so beautiful, but he wasn't ready to approach her in that way yet. There was too much going on at that moment, with him trying to settle into his new life. He was adjusting to the band—Rayne already had them in the studio laying down tracks and was planning to send them around to the local stations to get some airtime. He was still learning his way around the city, trying to find an apartment he could afford. As if matters weren't enough, the credit card companies were giving him a hard time about sending his cards to the hotel because it was not a permanent address. So, even if he were lucky enough to find a great apartment he had no way of putting down a deposit.

With his life in transition, Tristan understood that now was not the time to attempt to start a new relationship. Especially not with a woman like Rayne. She was the kind of woman who would demand a man's full attention, and he wanted to be able to give it to her. He wanted to be able to wine and dine her properly and, when the time was right, have a decent apartment to bring her back to.

"Come on." She leaned into him and Tristan resisted the temptation to meet her halfway. "I'll pay," she whispered.

Tristan chuckled. "No, thanks. You need to get going before *you* get sick." He gestured to a cab parked not far away.

When the cab pulled to the curb, he opened the door for Rayne and she turned to him again, still holding her open umbrella. "Tristan, I insist. There is no reason for you to be out here in the rain. Where do you live?"

"Not far from here."

"Then what's the problem? It will be a short ride." She closed the umbrella and climbed into the cab. Scooting over, she patted the seat next to her.

In his mind, Tristan saw her climbing into bed and patting

the space next to her welcoming him in. He shook his head to get rid of the image. He was just about to tell her *no* one final time when she tilted her head to the side in the most provocative way he'd ever seen. Looking up at him with her sultry bedroom eyes, she quietly threw his words back at him.

"What are you afraid of?"

That did it. Tristan smiled and climbed into the cab beside her. He gave the driver an address one street over from the motel, figuring he'd get out and walk the rest of the way without Rayne any the wiser. But as soon as the cab came to a stop, Rayne took one look around and shook her head.

"This will never do." She knocked on the glass and gave the driver another address.

Before Tristan could open the door, the car was pulling away from the curb.

"Hey!" He turned in the seat to face her. "What are you doing?"

Her eyes narrowed in on his face. "I know you just moved here from Albany, but that neighborhood is nothing more than a tourist trap known for its pickpockets and con men."

"Yeah. So what?"

"I told you I have a low tolerance for bull, Tristan. If you're down on your luck—that's okay. But don't try to jerk me around."

"What are you talking about?"

"According to you, you've been in the city for two weeks. Why haven't you found an apartment? Why are you still living in a hotel? If you couldn't afford a place you should've just said so."

Tristan laid his head back on the seat and sighed. "I was robbed my first day here. They got almost everything. My luggage, most of my money. I just didn't want to have to call my family for help, so I was staying where I could afford.

And to top it off, my credit card companies are giving me a hard time, so who knows how long it will take me to get replacements."

"Why didn't you say something sooner?"

"What was there to say?" He glanced out the window. "Where are we going?"

"My place. You can stay with me for now."

He sat straight up in his seat. "Rayne, there is no way I could impose on you like that. I mean, it's a really kind offer, but I couldn't—"

That sandy eyebrow rose in an expression he was coming to know well. "Tristan, that wasn't a question. I now have a vested interest in your health and safety. And I'm not about to let you keep creeping around there until something worse than a mugging happens to you." She winked. "Don't worry, my place is plenty big enough for the both of us."

A few minutes later the cab pulled up in front of a tall apartment building and Tristan, who was starting to feel the exhaustion of the night come down on him, followed Rayne inside.

They stepped off on the eighteenth floor and he followed her down a plush hallway to her apartment. As they entered, Tristan's eyes were immediately drawn to the stark white walls decorated with black-and-white prints.

It took all of five seconds for him to realize the prints were erotic paintings. As Rayne moved around him, taking off her jacket, hanging up the umbrella and dropping her mail on the small white desk that sat in the corner, Tristan was left with nothing to do but stand and stare.

"You didn't strike me as the type to be easily shocked." He turned to where her voice was coming from, the kitchenette. She was taking something out of the refrigerator.

"I'm not usually." He forced his eyes away from the artwork to the white leather multisectional sofa that took up a large portion of the big room. There was a white marble round dining table and white shag rugs throughout the room.

*Looks as if someone got stuck in the seventies,* Tristan thought. The decor looked like something straight out of a James Bond movie. Strangely, the decor matched her personality.

"Care for something to eat?" She lifted a small white box of what was obviously leftover takeout Chinese food.

"No, thanks," he said, moving toward the hallway leading to the back rooms. "If I eat that stuff now, I'll be up until noon." He stopped at the entrance of the brightly colored hallway. The two walls were painted mustard yellow and lined with pictures of Rayne with various celebrities and friends—mostly men—at different stages of her life. Some of the pictures left little doubt as to the relationships she'd shared with some of the men.

With a frown he turned to the lab-white living room lined with provocative art and then turned back to the cozy hallway. Both were Rayne, both suited her and together they revealed facets to her that he'd yet to realize.

*Maybe this living-together thing is not such a bad idea,* he thought.

She passed him in the hall, carrying a steaming plate of shrimp fried rice.

"Here's your room." The next doorway she came to, she paused. "There are extra blankets in the closet if you get cold." With a yawn, she turned and headed farther down the hall to the last doorway on the left. "Get some sleep and we'll work out the details of this later. Okay?"

Tristan nodded and without another word she disappeared into the room.

Tristan entered the bedroom that was modernly decorated in forest greens and gold. He was surprised to see the room had its own private bath. He set his guitar and backpack on the floor and sat down on the side of the plush bed.

Rayne Phillips was one of the most unusual people he'd ever met. Like the living room and the hallway, everything about her seemed to be a contradiction. She seemed street-smart, and yet she'd brought home a man she barely knew like some kind of stray dog.

For a week he'd been watching her, observing almost everything she did as she moved around the club day to day taking care of her enterprises. He couldn't help it. Something about her drew his attention like a moth to a flame and it had been that way from the first moment he heard her voice.

He wanted her. With every fiber of his being he wanted her. He wanted her like he hadn't wanted a woman in years. But he also wanted any relationship with Rayne to be something more than what she was apparently used to. He now knew he wanted to be more than just another picture on her hallway walls.

Up until then, he'd had no idea how to make that happen. In the short time he worked for her, he'd already picked up on Rayne's free-spirited attitudes toward life and sex. And thanks to the guys, he'd learned a lot about the men who'd come before him.

None of it boded well for his situation. According to Dex, Rayne had this set of rules she lived by. Nothing she verbalized constantly, but over time those close to her picked up on them.

For instance, after a fling that turned into a stalking situation with a previous guitarist, Rayne no longer dated musicians, especially those that worked for her. And after a close call with a college student who purchased an engagement ring after two nights in her bed, she steered away from younger men. Although there were only five years between them, he thought that still might present a problem for Rayne.

And, according to Ronnie, after her last serious relationship, the one with music producer Melvin Ferrell, ended badly, Rayne made some adjustments in the types of men she dated. Now she preferred the typical boy toy and "open" relationships.

That whole "open" relationship thing was completely out of the question in Tristan's mind. There was no way he was going to be okay with his woman going out with other men.

He took off his shoes and stretched out across the bed. Based on what he knew about her so far, the idea of having any kind of serious relationship with her seemed close to impossible. But, then again, here he was lying in a bed in her home.

The night's exhaustion finally won. As Tristan closed his eyes his final thought was the memory of Rayne in the cab, tilting her head to the side and patting the seat next to her. This time when the image of her sitting in bed beckoning him to her came to his mind he didn't push it away.

The next morning, as promised, he and Rayne discussed their living arrangement over coffee and Danish. In her typical businesslike fashion, she offered him a renter/tenant agreement. She would reduce his weekly pay by the amount he was paying for renting the hotel room and he would help out with chores around the apartment. Apparently, she hated housework.

Tristan accepted the offer on the condition that Rayne understood it was only until he received his credit cards and was able to find a place of his own. Although considering she held this discussion with him while she was wearing a sheer pink teddy, Tristan thought it was a wonder he was able to remember anything she'd said.

That afternoon, he went back to the hotel and collected his few possessions. He packed up the few clothes he'd purchased after losing all of his and his few toiletries and checked out.

Within a few days the pair had settled into a comfortable routine, and surprisingly enough, discovered they made pretty good roommates.

In the morning, they had breakfast together and then Rayne left for the club while Tristan cleaned up and got in some writing time. In the evenings, Tristan helped Rayne close up the club and they caught a cab home together. But the best part was the in-between times. Often, one of them would bring up a seemingly innocuous conversation and they would end up spending hours in deep discussion over some of the most painful and happy moments of their lives.

The only downside for Tristan was the secret fear that she would one day bring home a man and all hell would break loose. Because he did not see how he could stand by and watch her go into her bedroom with another man. But after two weeks of no one at all coming to the apartment, Tristan began to think that maybe the guys had exaggerated about her love life.

"This has been the wettest summer I can remember," Rayne said, standing at the window one Saturday morning as the pouring rain pelted the apartment.

Tristan sat at the small desk with a pencil between his lips as he thumped out the latest chord of a song he was working on. "What's that?"

She stretched and came over to where he was sitting. "I said it's wet out there. What are you working on?" She leaned over the back of the white leather desk chair to see the sheet of music on the desk.

"Tell me what you think," he said before strumming out the half-written song. When he finished, he looked up to find her looking at him with a strange expression.

"I could spend my life listening to you sing," she whispered.

The atmosphere in the room seemed suddenly heavy, as if

she'd said so much more than the few spoken words. Realizing she'd crossed some unseen boundary, Rayne stood straight and cleared her throat. "I like it. What's it called?"

He smiled and shrugged. "Don't know yet."

"It's very soulful…and a little sad."

"I know." He nodded, still strumming a few notes. "I can't control how a song comes to me. Sometimes I'll sit down to write a ballad and end up with something hip-hop. Then again, I'll be all charged about a beat—a fast tempo beat in my head, but when I get it on paper it's something like this."

"Was this one of those songs you heard in your head?"

He nodded, continuing to play. Suddenly he stopped. "But I only hear it when I'm near you."

He glanced up at her and their eyes locked for several long moments, neither willing to look away and break the connection and both afraid of where it was all leading.

Finally, Rayne forced herself to turn away. She crossed the room and flopped down on the sofa.

Taking her cue, Tristan forced his attention back to the guitar in his hands and the song in his mind. He strummed a few more random notes and asked again, "But you do like it?"

A soft smile spread to a wide grin on Rayne's face. "I love it. How could I not?" She clamped her hands together. "Okay, let me hear it again—this time, from the top."

Tristan played the song once more, this time trying to convey all the emotion he'd felt writing it, trying to tell her with his music what she'd come to mean to him.

"Whoa," she said with a heavy sigh once he was finished. "I can't believe it has taken you so long to get serious about your music, but at the same time I'm glad it did because we wouldn't have met otherwise."

"What did you call it?" he asked, leaning his elbow on his guitar as he searched his memory.

"Providence."

"That's right. Providence. It's sorta like fate, huh?"

"I'm a firm believer in providence. There is no such thing as coincidence."

He stared into her eyes. "You really believe that?"

Her eyes widened. "Of course. Don't you?"

"I don't know. But what makes you think I would?"

"Well, it takes a pretty strong dose of faith to give up your stable life and try something altogether different."

"It's not exactly different. I did play clubs in Albany."

"But you always knew that if it didn't work out, you had your day job to fall back on."

"I still do."

She shook her head. "No, it won't be the same now."

"You don't think so?" he asked.

"Try to think back to your last day at the school. Try to remember how that felt. And then consider how you feel today. Everything you've gone through since then."

"I see what you mean, maybe it wouldn't be the same—but I could do it if I had to."

"But you won't have to."

"What makes you so sure?"

She glanced at him with a devilish gleam in her eyes. "Well…I wasn't going to say anything just yet, but Melvin is bringing a couple of his scouts by to hear you guys next week."

"Already?"

"Tristan, you have to strike while the iron is hot and you guys are on fire! The word is really getting around town about Optimus Five. You're the hottest thing going right now, and I want us to take full advantage of that while we can."

Tristan put his guitar to the side and leaned forward in the chair. "Rayne, not to sound ungrateful, but we've only been playing together for a couple of weeks. Don't you think you're moving a little fast?"

"No, Tristan, *you've* only been playing with the band for a couple of weeks. The others have been waiting for this opportunity forever. You were the missing piece and now that we have you, why wait? And isn't this what you came to New York for?"

"I guess so. I just didn't expect everything to happen so fast."

Rayne stood from the sofa and crossed the room to kneel before Tristan. Taking his hands in hers, she looked him directly in the eyes. "You know that old cliché about how opportunity only knocks once? It's true, Tristan. I know from firsthand experience. When the moment is right, you only get one chance to make it happen. This is your moment."

Tristan stared back, seeing deeper than Rayne knew. "You're talking about your acting career, aren't you?"

She sat back on her heels. "Yes."

"Do you mind if I ask what happened?"

Rayne sat silently staring down at her hands where they rested on her thighs for so long Tristan was certain she wouldn't answer. He was preparing to stand up when she finally spoke.

"My mother happened." She looked up at him. "I was betrayed by the one person who was supposed to take care of me."

Tristan slid out of the chair to sit next to her on the floor, his legs tucked beneath him. He said nothing, simply waited for her to continue.

Finally she did. "She started putting me in commercials before I could walk. For the first fifteen years of my life, I worked almost nonstop." She looked at him and for the first time, he saw tears in her pretty eyes. "I worked my whole life and she took everything. She spent every dime of my money that was required by law to be put in a trust because I was underaged. But she was the trustee."

Not knowing what else to do, Tristan reached out and pulled her into his arms. "I'm sorry, I didn't mean to bring up bad memories." He smoothed her hair back away from her face as she gave in to the tears.

"I try not to think about it too often. About how different life would've been for me if she had not done what she did. But sometimes it just all comes rushing back." She reached up and wrapped her arms around his neck, and Tristan knew he could not have stopped what came next.

"Shh." Leaning her back against the carpet, he covered her mouth with his mouth, rolled over and covered her body, as well. "Don't think about it. Think about this." Slowly, he kissed along her neckline, savoring her smell, the feel of her soft skin against his lips. He'd wanted this from the moment he met her and now she was here, in his arms, and it was better than he'd imagined it would feel.

Letting his hands roam over her body, Tristan slowly unbuttoned the pajama top revealing the twin mounds that haunted his dreams. "You're so beautiful," he whispered, finding himself in awe of her perfection.

Rayne reached up and pulled his head to her breast, silently telling him what she wanted and Tristan was more than happy to oblige. Her busy hands found their way inside his T-shirt, pulling and tugging and he quickly pulled it over his head, bringing them flesh to flesh for the first time.

The feel of her hardened nipples against his bare skin was almost enough to send him over the edge, but he held back. Moving from over her, he leaned up on one elbow and looked at the half-naked woman in his arms. Her lips swollen with his kisses, her eyes dazed with lust and...vulnerability.

*What am I doing?* Tristan sat up suddenly. "I'm sorry, I

had no right. I—" He stood and hurried down the hall to his bedroom. He went straight into the bathroom to the sink and, turning on the cold water, splashed his face repeatedly trying to cool his burning blood.

Tristan had wanted Rayne for what seemed like an eternity, but not like this, not when she was in such a vulnerable state. He closed his eyes and took several deep breaths, trying to regain some control over himself.

Suddenly, he felt warm, gentle hands sliding over his rib cage as she pressed herself against his back.

Tristan felt his slow heartbeat begin to accelerate once again as her busy fingers continued their exploration of his body. Using all the willpower he could muster, Tristan covered her hands to stop their slow progression, opened his eyes and looked at her beautiful reflection in the mirror.

As if sensing his question, Rayne said, "Tristan, I know what I'm doing. I want you."

He knew he was only holding on to his self-control by the thinnest thread; his dark eyes pierced hers in the mirror. "Are you sure?"

Her answer was to lean up and run her tongue over his earlobe. In an instant, Tristan had swooped her up in his arms and carried her to his bed. Maybe it was wrong, he thought, but he wouldn't ask twice.

Without thought of the consequences, with no care for what tomorrow would bring them, he slid her pajama pants down her legs, pleasantly surprised to see she did not sleep in underwear. For a brief moment, he wondered if she slept in pajamas at all. The loose-fitting, cotton sleepwear had seemed out of place on her from the first time he saw her in it and now he wondered if she wore them for his benefit. After tonight, he thought, he would burn the damn things.

Gently, his hand found its way up her long calf and her athletic thigh, to the center of her womanhood and he almost shouted when he realized she was wet for him already. Her body was as prepared as it would ever be.

Tristan sat back and quickly disrobed, and with a fluid motion he guided himself inside her body. Taking a deep breath as the hot opening enveloped him, slowly giving way to his size until he was planted deep inside her.

Rayne felt as if the whole world was spinning as she held on to his shoulders. Her breathing had become shallow as she struggled to hold off on her release.

Finally! Her aching body had craved this man for so long, but she'd fought the hunger for all the reasons life had taught her. He was too young. He was a musician and her employee… and as of late, he'd become her friend. She didn't want to jeopardize all of that for the hot sex she knew they would have together.

But, now that he was inside her, all those reasons seemed ridiculous. How much longer could she have resisted this? Slowly, he began to move inside her, lifting her legs over his thighs, opening her, and it was simply all she could do to hold on to his broad shoulder and bury her head against his neck to keep from crying out in pleasure.

He felt so right. More right than anything she had felt in a very long time. What he was doing to her, she felt in every part of her body. It wasn't the typical quick, physical release, but more like a downpour of the ultimate gratification.

She clutched his shoulders as the soft moan escaped her lips, her mouth on his neck, on his cheek, searching for his lips so she could tell him with her kiss what she knew in her heart. This was not just two people having sex, this was a bonding, a connecting, and neither of them would be the same afterward.

Tristan broke the kiss long enough to whisper in her ear, "Let it go, baby. Give it to me."

Unable to deny him anything, Rayne felt her whole body

vibrating with an uncontrollable wildness as orgasm after orgasm took her over. Soon she felt Tristan's arms tighten around her as his essence filled her and he followed her over the edge.

# Chapter 5

After that afternoon, things seem to fall into place so quickly, Tristan was left with his head spinning. He and Rayne became inseparable outside of the club, but somehow they managed to keep the interaction at work on a strictly professional level.

Tristan finally gave in to the credit card companies and asked them to send the cards to his parents' home, which was one of the addresses they had on file. Which meant he had to let his family know that he'd *lost* his cards. Giving as little detail as possible he explained that he'd moved in with a friend and asked that they forward the cards to the address he gave.

When they weren't working or making love, Tristan and Rayne were seeing the sights of New York. Despite her previous objections to his hotel, Rayne seemed determined to take Tristan to every tourist trap in the city. He silently wondered if it was some kind of new New Yorker initiation.

And regardless of the fact that they talked to each other

constantly, they never seemed to run out of conversation. Tristan told her all about his close-knit family and how they had, for the most part, supported his desire to pursue his music. He told her about the kids he taught and the pleasure he'd found in teaching.

Rayne told him about her experiences as a child actress, both good and bad. Like the fun in being famous and having people eager to fulfill your every wish. But she also shared the painful experiences of being her mother's daughter.

Monique Phillips had burned more than her fair share of bridges over the years with little regard for how her actions affected her daughter. Everything from repeatedly having affairs with the commercial directors to demanding script rewrites. But when the affairs went sour or the producers got fed up with Monique's ridiculous requests it was Rayne who was canned, not her mother.

And despite Monique constantly dragging her from one audition to the next, the pair still spent most of Rayne's childhood living hand to mouth. As Rayne grew older and began to mature, Monique seemed to become more desperate, lying about her age to producers, forcing her to tape down her budding breasts until there was no way to deny she was becoming a woman. Monique acted as if by maturing Rayne was somehow being deliberately defiant. Her antics and demands grew more and more outrageous until anyone considering using the beautiful girl-child with the sweet disposition in their commercials shied away at the prospect of dealing with her psychotic mother. In other words, by the time Rayne was able to take control of her own career, her professional reputation had already been destroyed.

One quiet Sunday afternoon, as they were walking along an avenue not far from Rayne's apartment, something in a shop window caught Rayne's eye. She stopped and peered at the little dragon amulet.

Tristan came up beside her to see what had caught her eye. "What's with you and dragons?"

She shrugged. "I just like mythical creatures."

"You are a mythical creature."

She smiled at him over her shoulders. "What's that supposed to mean?"

"Just that you're like magic," he said wistfully, studying her profile as she continued to examine the pieces in the display.

"No more magical than gorgeous lead singers who show up out of nowhere."

His mouth twisted in a smirk. "I know it's not the big city, but Albany is not exactly nowhere. And I didn't just show up—I answered your ad in the newspaper."

"Shush! Stop trying to ruin my fantasy."

For some reason the statement struck him as odd. Tristan turned her to face him. "I'm no fantasy. No mythical creature who's just going to disappear when you're done with him. I'm real, Rayne. And I plan to stay."

She looked into his eyes as if trying to determine his sincerity. Then, without a word, she turned back to the window to continue examining the displays.

He noticed a beautiful yellow diamond solitaire had caught her eye. He wasn't surprised. The window was lined with perfect traditional white diamonds in typical settings and various other stones. But the yellow diamond was by far the most unique thing in the window, just like everything about Rayne.

"That would make a beautiful engagement ring," he said quietly.

She stood straight up as if he'd just poked her in the spine. "Or a nice centerpiece in a tiara." She turned with a huge smile, holding her hands over her head in the shape of an invisible tiara. "What do you think?"

*I think you're ducking the subject—again,* Tristan thought, but simply smiled instead. "Princess Rayne, I like it."

Together they continued down the avenue, each lost to their own thoughts.

Tristan was remembering exactly why he never broached the subject of their future. They never made plans beyond where to eat at night, but Tristan accepted it because he understood Rayne would need time to get used to the idea of a committed relationship. He wasn't worried because when they were at the club or out in public she showed no interest in other men.

Rayne, on the other hand, was hoping and praying he never said anything like that again. She was not the marrying type, and her relationship with Tristan was so perfect as it was, she had no desire to end it this soon. If he started talking marriage she would have to. One of the few lessons Monique had been successful in teaching her daughter was that there is no such thing as happily-ever-after, only heartbreak and disappointment, and those were not emotions she ever wanted to associate with Tristan.

Tristan soon discovered there were other benefits of his new relationship with Rayne. His musical creativity blossomed like a rose in the sun. He began to write complete songs in one sitting, and each of them revolved around Rayne and how she made him feel. He would play the new songs for her and she would listen with rapt attention.

Although he never found the perfect title for the nameless ballad he had written, Rayne loved the song so much she asked him to play it for her almost every day. Tristan played the song so much he began to think of it as their theme song. He called it "Beats of My Heart," as his own secret reference to the woman who inspired it.

Later than expected, but as promised, Mel Ferrell showed

up with two talent scouts. Tristan had not known who the man was at first, but the guys quickly filled him in.

They had been practicing some of Tristan's music for a while, so when he launched into one of the never-before-heard songs the crowd went wild and their energy infused the band, which ended up playing better than they ever had before.

The scouts were impressed. They could see it in the looks the men exchanged and the notes that were being taken.

After their performance, Mel came to the stage to shake everyone's hand and Tristan tried to push the knowledge that this man was Rayne's former lover from his mind. He tried to focus solely on what Mel Ferrell could do for Optimus Five.

That night when he and Rayne made love, he poured all the passion and fears of his heart into her body. Again and again, he took her to the pinnacle of pleasure, torturing her with his lips and hands. Sanity told him that the only threat Mel Ferrell presented was in his mind, but sanity had no place in the all-consuming affair with Rayne.

Mel Ferrell began coming around the club regularly, and he watched Tristan with undeniable interest. He arranged for the group to have a demo made, and brought them into the label headquarters for a formal audition.

The whole experience was mind-blowing for Tristan, considering it had only been a matter of weeks since he'd left Albany. But nothing compared to the first time he and the guys heard their first single track being played by a local station.

There had been no warning, they were sitting around the bar one afternoon before rehearsal working out the set for each night of the week. The radio had been playing low in the background and then the DJ had announced he wanted callers to let him know if the next song was a hit or not.

The next song was written by Tristan Daniels and played by Optimus Five. As soon as he realized what he was hearing he rushed down the hallway to Rayne's office and scooped her up in his arms.

"What was that about?" She laughed as he sat her back on her feet; in answer Tristan crossed behind her desk and tuned her radio to the right station.

Her eyes widened in amazement before she rushed back across the room and straight into his arms. "I told you! I told you!" She planted kisses all over his face, not caring who might walk in.

Once the track hit the airwaves, the line to get into Optimus every night grew three blocks. Everyone wanted to see the band and their hot new lead singer. And the women came out of the woodwork. Everywhere he turned, Tristan was being bombarded by offers and invitations, some of which would've been very tempting if he had not already fallen in love with a superheroine.

With each passing day, Tristan was more and more sure that was exactly what she was. Because she had taken his staid life and turned it on its head in a way only someone with magical powers could. She'd fulfilled his lifelong dream and given him love, as well.

Despite his certainty that he would spend his life with Rayne, Tristan never mentioned her to his family. Being his family, he knew they would want to meet Rayne right away and he just wasn't sure she was ready to deal with that yet. He did, however, keep them completely up-to-date on his music and they were all impressed to hear that his single was being played on local stations.

For the moment Tristan was content to just allow things to continue on as they had, certain that they had time. They were young and in love and everything in their universe seemed to be moving in perfect harmony.

But what Tristan did not realize was that his perfect harmony was terrifying Rayne. It hadn't taken her long to realize that whatever she was doing with Tristan was different than anything she'd ever been in before.

She kept trying to tell herself it was just another love affair, but that was just what she was telling herself. In the morning, she awoke looking for him and did not breathe until she found him, usually sound asleep beside her.

When he sang, she listened with an almost trancelike devotion, feeling a woman's pride in his lyrics of love and passion. She loved the way her apartment smelled because he lived there. She loved the way he brought her flowers almost every day. She loved the way he looked at her. Lord—how she loved the way he loved her.

Even when they were at the club and both working, he would glance at her, just a glance. And with that one glance convey all his wonderfully decadent thoughts of what he planned to do with her when they got home.

She'd never been in a relationship like this before. She'd never felt this kind of intensity for someone. And all these firsts were terrifying.

Usually Rayne went into a new relationship knowing when and how it would end. She knew these things because she was the one who decided them. Usually she was in complete control, but with Tristan that control was completely gone.

All he had to do was touch her and she fell into his lap like an eager harem girl. All he had to do was form the word *Rayne* on his lips and she was by his side. But worst of all, she'd come to depend on him and even in her confused state she knew that was a definite *no-no*. Dependence bred vulnerability and she had not been vulnerable since she was fifteen years old.

Dependence also tended to make a person think long-term. And Rayne Phillips did not do long-term. It was the one quality she happily took from her mother's repertoire.

Whatever was going on between her and Tristan had to stay on the surface level. But even as she told herself that, she knew it was already too late. He'd gotten under her skin and was fast taking over her heart.

One evening, almost three weeks into their relationship, Tristan came back from a trip to the fruit market down the street to find Rayne had spread out a blanket on the living-room floor and lit candles around the room.

When he entered she was sitting cross-legged in the middle of the blanket. Tristan looked around the room in confusion. "Umm…" He shook his head not sure how to form the question in his mind.

Rayne sat up a little straighter. "I want to read your aura."

"Say what?" He frowned at her, wondering if maybe she'd been dipping into that claret she liked so much while he was gone.

"Just come here, but take off your shoes first."

"Rayne, I need to put this fruit up."

"This is more important."

"Reading my aura is more important than overripe bananas? I don't think so."

She tilted her head to the side. "I know you think I'm a flake, but I'm serious about this. Just come here."

With a shake of his head, Tristan set the bag down on the small desk and slipped off his loafers. "You are a flake, but lucky for you, you're a beautiful flake."

He sat down across from her and folded his legs to match hers. "Now what?"

"Give me your hands."

He stretched his hands out and Rayne gently wrapped them in her own, rubbing her thumbs over his palm pads.

He closed his eyes. "Hmm…I think I can get to like this aura thing."

"Shh," she scolded while continuing to rub his palms. "You have a lot of green in your aura."

"What's green stand for? A virile sex drive?"

"No, green is compassion—and sensitivity. Which makes sense given that you're a musician."

"Sensitivity? What color represents virile sex drive?"

She laughed. "No color is designated for sex drives. It doesn't work like that." She stared at him for several long seconds. "And blue, a lot of blue."

"Blue is a good color. Blue is a manly man color."

"Actually, blue represents a calm nature."

Tristan snatched his hands back. "Okay, enough of this." He started to stand. "This aura thing is making me out to be a wimp."

She sat looking up at him. "You're no wimp."

"I'm glad you recognized that," he said in mock offense. He picked up the bag of fruit and headed to the kitchen. He had half emptied the bag before he realized Rayne had been completely quiet the whole time.

"What's wrong?"

She shrugged. "Nothing. It's just my aura is so different from yours."

"Haven't you heard? Opposites attract."

"But can they hold?"

"What's that supposed to mean?"

She shook her head as if to throw off some unpleasant thought. "Nothing." She stood. "What do you want for dinner?"

"Hey, wait a minute." He crossed the room to her. "That was just a game, right?"

She simply stared at him.

"Rayne, you can't seriously give that whole aura thing any validity."

She smiled. "You're right. So, where are we eating?"

Tristan wondered briefly if he should pursue the topic because he felt in his gut that she was indeed taking it seriously. But he decided that maybe if they went out to dinner it would serve as a good distraction.

He named their favorite Italian restaurant and within an hour they were seated and ordering their dinner. The conversation had turned to the band and Mel Ferrell's involvement, but all evening Tristan could not shake the belief that Rayne was still holding on to the earlier events.

## *Chapter 6*

Thinking he was dreaming, Tristan ignored the ringing bell until reality broke through his sleepy haze and he realized it was the front doorbell.

"Who the hell could that be, this time of the morning?" His mumbled words were directed at Rayne, whose only answer was to shift onto her side and pull the covers closer around her body.

With a yawn and a frown, Tristan dragged his feet over the side of the bed, seeing how Rayne had made it perfectly clear *she* would *not* be answering the door.

He slipped into his boxers lying on the floor by the bed and rubbing his eyes he stumbled to the front door. "Who is it?"

"Tristan? It's Mom."

"Mom?" That one word brought him fully awake. He looked through the peephole in the door and his eyes widened to see his entire family standing there. Not only his mother and father but Tracy and Calvin, as well.

He quickly unlocked the door, his mind racing with the possibilities of what major, catastrophic event would bring his whole family to the city. He briefly wondered how they knew where to find him, and then remembered giving the address to his mom to forward his credit cards.

"What's wrong?" he asked as the door swung open and his family poured into Rayne's living room. Katherine smiled up at her son. "Nothing's wrong. Does something have to be wrong for me to visit my only son?"

Tristan only frowned at his mother, his sleepy mind now completely befuddled. He glanced at the clock on the kitchen wall and saw that it was 10:32 a.m.

He realized that Calvin had noticed the artwork on the walls when he saw him whispering something to Tracy. Her eyes quickly darted over the walls, a slightly confused expression crinkled her brow.

"Don't I get a hug?" Kate asked, her eyes taking in every inch of the apartment.

Instinctively, Tristan hugged his mother and father, still trying to understand exactly what was happening. "So nothing's wrong—why didn't you tell me you were coming?"

"Wouldn't have been much of a surprise, now would it?" Tracy said, her mind still distracted by the pictures.

"Surprise!" Kate raised her arms in a grand gesture and winked at her son just before Tracy leaned forward and whispered something in her ear.

Kate's attention was called to the erotic art that decorated the apartment. "Oh, my," she whispered, and Tristan only then remembered the woman sleeping in the other room and what an awkward situation he was now in. Oh, well, he thought, they were going to find out sooner or later. He'd just hoped to have time to solidify his relationship with Rayne and introduce them at an appropriate time and place. Like dinner in a restaurant—where everyone was fully dressed.

His father put his arm around Tristan's shoulders. "We're here to take you out to breakfast to celebrate your new single. We heard it on the radio, just the other day!"

"Ben, look," Katherine whispered and tugged her husband's arm, pointing at a black-and-white print taken directly from the *Kama Sutra*.

Tristan was beginning to understand why his family was here now and wanted to kick himself for not anticipating this development. His family was incredibly supportive of each other. Of course they would want to celebrate his recent success with him. He just wished they would've given him some notice.

Tristan watched with a pained expression as his father pulled his reading glasses from his shirt pocket and propped them on the tip of his nose. He stood mute as his father examined the pictures closer, but all he wanted to do was run around the room and tear each of them down. He knew assumptions would be made and opinions formed before any of them even had a chance to get to know Rayne and realize what a wonderful woman she was.

Just as he expected, Ben made no comment, but an expression was worth a thousand words.

"I really wish you would've called," Tristan said, shaking his head and trying to decide how to move forward. Should he get them out of the apartment and into a hotel before Rayne awoke? Or wake Rayne and get the introductions over with?

Tracy was wandering across the room as if drawn by some magnetic force and she was headed directly toward the most flagrant display of them all. At first glance the picture appeared to be just two shadowy figures intertwined until the eyes adjusted and the figure became *several human bodies sexually connected*. Tristan thought there was much to be said for Rayne's stylishly unique apartment, but the artwork was designed to catch everyone's immediate attention. Just as Rayne wanted it to.

"Look, something I need to tell you."

He directed his attention to his mother.

"Tristan!" Tracy's high-pitched voice could've awakened the dead, and Tristan knew instantly the time for his family making a discreet retreat had passed. "What have you gotten yourself into here?"

"Something I've only dreamed about," Calvin muttered, but in the sudden quiet of the room, everyone heard.

"Are you rooming with someone, son?" Ben finally asked.

"You could say that." Tristan took a deep breath. "Remember me telling you that—"

"Tristan?" The one word, spoken so softly, had a hundred questions wrapped in it. Tristan turned to Rayne standing in the bedroom door, dressed in her emerald robe.

Her long gold-tinted hair fell in a tangled mess around her small face. Even in her disheveled state, she was the most beautiful woman he'd ever seen and he was so proud to call her his own.

He smiled. "My family wanted to surprise me—and they did." He walked across the room to her and put his arm around her waist, bringing her forward.

"Everyone, this is Rayne. Rayne, this is my sister, Tracy, and her husband, Calvin, my father, Ben, and my moth—"

Tristan stopped short, seeing the look of horror on his mother's face. She stared at Rayne with the most hate he'd ever seen in her eyes. His loving, gentle-natured mother looked like a tigress ready to attack.

"Mom, what's wrong?"

Still staring at Rayne, her eyes narrowed as she moved

forward. And as if sensing danger, Rayne moved backward out of Tristan's arm.

"What did you say your name was?" Katherine asked, stopping within a foot of Rayne.

"She didn't." Tristan stepped back and recaptured Rayne's waist, knowing on some unspoken emotional level that she needed his touch now. "Mom, what's going on?"

Katherine shook her head as if confused. "You're *too young,* it's not possible. Of course, I wouldn't put it past her to make a deal with the devil for eternal youth!"

Tristan could only watch as his mother's eyes ran over every inch of Rayne's face as if searching for some hidden message, some hint of recognition.

He had no idea what was going on or what would come next. "What is this about?"

Tristan looked first at his mother and then glanced at Rayne, surprised by the look of resignation on her face. In that moment, he realized Rayne was more aware of what was happening here than he was. But how? He was almost certain the two women had never met. Yet they seemed locked in some kind of time warp together where the only two people they could see were each other.

Feeling helpless, Tristan turned to his father. "Dad? Do you understand what's going on here?"

In his peripheral vision, he could see Tracy and Calvin standing off to the side, watching the events unfold and looking as confused as he felt.

"It's not her, Katie." Ben came up behind his wife and pulled her against his side. He, too, was staring at Rayne as if he'd seen a ghost. "But, my God, she's her spitting image."

"Who the hell are you talking about?" Tristan finally lost his temper. He needed answers. "What is going on?"

Rayne looked at him and only then did he see the tears

in her eyes. "My mother, Tristan. She's talking about my mother."

*"Monique Phillips."* Katherine said the word as if it were the foulest thing she'd ever uttered. "That's your mother, isn't it?"

"Yes." Rayne uttered the one word as if it held the greatest shame imaginable.

Tracy's gasp was the only sound heard before Tristan's mind was instantly flooded with the stories of a lifetime. *Monique Phillips? Rayne Phillips. How could I have not made the connection?*

Tristan could see the memories running over his mother, as well. Now standing before her was the daughter of Monique Phillips, the woman's spitting image. Tristan knew that Rayne was just another victim of Monique's conniving and manipulation, but Kate had no way of knowing that. All she saw was the very image of her nemesis, and her son was holding on to the younger woman as if she belonged to him.

Tristan watched as his mother's eyes floated down to where his arm was clutched around Rayne's small waist. As her eyes came back up to meet his he watched as the feral rage in them turned to sorrow.

"Tristan?" Kate clutched her stomach as if in pain. "Are you and this woman…"

Tristan could feel the storm building in the room, the air was literally becoming thinner, oppressive, and he knew with soul certainty that if he did not stop it now things were about to spiral out of control.

"Mom, this is Rayne—not Monique. This is the woman I love. You can't hold her responsible for the actions of her mother."

"If you don't mind me asking," Ben said, still holding his wife against his side, "how did you two meet?"

Rayne spoke for the first time. "I own a nightclub. Tristan auditioned for my band."

"So…you're his *boss?*" Ben looked slightly taken aback by the revelation.

"Wait a minute!" Tracy's high-pitched squeak came from across the room.

"Tracy, stay out of this," Calvin said. "This has nothing to do with us."

"Oh, hell, no!" She moved across the room quickly and Tristan instantly blocked her path. "Surely you don't think this is some kind of coincidence?" She stared up at her little brother in amazement. "Don't you see? She's going to do the same thing to you that her mother did to ours."

"Tracy, back off." Tristan's tone was low and held a warning, and the look on Tracy's face told him she knew he was serious. "Please, everyone, let's just calm down." Tristan gestured to the white leather sofa.

"I'm not sitting on that thing." Tracy glanced around the walls again. "Who knows what's been going on up in here." She turned narrow eyes on her brother. "And I'm more than a little surprised that you're here, Tristan, sleeping with the enemy."

"Cut the dramatic crap, Tracy." He turned to face his mother. "Mom, Rayne and I are in love. I understand your history with her mother, but that's just it…history."

Katherine shook her head with something resembling pity. "You don't understand anything, son." She turned to the door. "I have to get out of here." She opened the door and hurried out with Ben following close behind.

He paused in the doorway, a troubled expression on his normally calm face. "Just give her some time, son. This has all come as a bit of a shock to her system."

As he left, Tracy and Calvin followed, saying nothing. Tracy simply stopped at the entrance to give Rayne one thorough dirty look and then they were all gone and the apartment was quiet once again.

They left the door standing wide-open, so Tristan crossed the room to close it. When he turned back, he saw that Rayne had returned to the bedroom.

He followed her in and saw her sitting on the side of the bed. He sat down beside her, taking her small hand in his. "I'm so sorry about that."

"What are the chances?" she whispered.

"That the son and daughter of two rivals would fall in love?" He chuckled, trying to make light of the situation. "I guess we are a real live Romeo and Juliet."

"And you see how that story ended." She pulled her hand away from his. "But that's not what I meant. It seems like every time I get something good, my mother finds a way to destroy it for me, even from the grave."

Something about the word *destroy* sent a chill down his spine. "I wouldn't go that far. I mean it was a bit awkward but nothing we can't handle."

She gave him a shocked expression. "A bit awkward? What planet are you living on?"

"Hey, I love my family, but they don't determine who I love." He lifted his hand and cupped her chin. "And I love you."

Rayne turned to look at him as she felt the emotional blockade fall into place with those three simple words. This was exactly what she had worked so hard to avoid all of her adult life.

Pain. Hurt. Fear.

She hadn't felt these emotions since she was a child and the decisions about her life were beyond her control. But she'd taken the reins at fifteen and never looked back and this was why! Those emotions were no less intense and debilitating today than they were all those years ago. How had she let things get this out of control?

She would never forget the hurt look on Tristan's face as his mother rushed out, or the paralyzing fear she'd felt believing he would follow. The hollow ache in the pit of her stomach in that moment was exactly the reason she avoided this kind of entanglement. After all, there was no fear of losing what you don't have.

"Did you hear me, Rayne?" Tristan held her stare, wanting her to see the truth in his words. "I said I love you." Tristan meant everything he'd said. He loved his family, but Rayne… Rayne was his future, his muse, and he wasn't about to let anything come between them. Not even a thirty-year-old feud.

Finally she smiled, but it was a stiff smile. "Hey, you're getting a little deep on me. I mean, this was fun, but love?"

He frowned. "What?"

"Come on, Tristan. I told you in the beginning that this was just a thing." She leaned forward and quickly kissed him. "A good thing, a hot thing, but just a thing."

Rayne stood from the bed and quickly wiped her eyes as if he were not supposed to see the tears forming there.

He stood, as well. "What are you doing? Are you trying to make this something little? Something that means nothing? It's not going to work, Rayne. It's too late. I love you and you love me. Don't deny it."

He tried to pull her into his arms but she backed up, putting her hands up in a defensive gesture.

"I told you in the beginning, I can't handle possessive men. I think you should go."

"Go? Go where? I live here, remember?"

She arched an eyebrow. "Not anymore." She folded her arms across her chest. "This was a mistake. You need to go."

Tristan simply stared at her dumbfounded, feeling as if he had somehow wandered into the twilight zone. "Okay, I admit, that was a bad scene." He gestured to the living room. "But they're gone now. It's nobody but you and me here. And up until about an hour ago, you and me were pretty damn good. Now you want me to go?"

"I'm sorry. If I had known you were getting clingy—"

"Clingy?"

"I thought you understood the rules."

"The rules? Woman, I love you! There are no rules in love!"

"This isn't love! This is hot sex and friendship. I don't do love!"

He could only laugh at the ridiculousness of the statement. "Well, you do a damn fine imitation of it."

"Get out, Tristan."

"So, you're throwing me away like all the others?"

Her eyes narrowed. "What made you think you were different?"

Tristan felt a sharp pain in his stomach as if she'd just plunged a knife into him. And in a way, she had.

"Okay…okay." The one word was all he could manage in his shocked state.

He turned to leave the room and stopped long enough to grab the jeans and shirt he'd worn the night before from the floor.

He crossed to the bathroom and dressed. When he came out, Rayne was gone. On the bed was her green robe, and he could see that she had hurriedly dressed. He wondered only briefly if his family had piled up and headed back to Albany. It didn't matter if they'd stayed in the city or returned home right away, the damage was done.

In the living room he walked over to the window and looked

down on the street for any sign of her. She was nowhere to be found, but he did see it had started raining. Pouring actually. Perfect weather, he thought, just perfect.

## *Chapter 7*

Rayne rushed along the busy avenue, feeling the pouring rain work its way beneath her thin jacket and plaster her hair to her skin and face. She had no umbrella and she didn't want one. She needed the rain to wash away the pain and anguish in her heart. She needed the rain to hide the tears that would not stop flowing down her face. Why did she always have to feel everything so intensely?

She ignored the curious stares of passersby and walked and walked and walked with absolutely no direction or destination. She walked wishing she could somehow walk through time and undo the past three months.

She wished she'd gone with her first instinct and rejected the sexy bass guitarist the minute he began to play. No, that wasn't true. Her time with Tristan had given her some of the best memories of her life. Memories she would always cherish and hold as precious jewels. But those times were over now. They had to be.

She thought back to the confrontation with his family that morning. Tristan was in the room, but apparently he'd completely missed the significance of what had occurred. His mother, whom Rayne knew he loved dearly, had rejected her as surely as if she'd said the words. And how could she not? This was the daughter of the woman she felt had ruined her career. And unfortunately Rayne looked so much like her mother that the memories of that betrayal would always be there between them. At every family gathering.

Pushing wet hair up off her forehead, she shivered with a chill. What was she thinking, family gatherings? There would be no family gatherings for her…ever. Family gatherings meant long-term commitment and that was a definite no-no. She never got attached, and when the men she dated did, she knew it was time to let them go.

Tristan was different, she'd known that almost from the start, but the rules she established for herself years ago had been set up for a reason. She laughed to herself. That reason had been to avoid situations like this. Finding herself wandering aimlessly through the city in the rain like a brokenhearted idiot. Until now, she'd always felt a slight contempt for women who allowed themselves to end up in this position. Crying over some man. She had never understood what could be so special about one man that could make a woman completely lose herself.

She got it now.

Growing up with a mother like Monique, Rayne had always been taught that *the one with the vagina ruled the game*. That was how Monique looked at relationships. A game.

But at the time Rayne was too young to understand that, and with the innocence of a child she developed filial affection for many of her mother's lovers. Most simply ignored her, but others were actually quite kind. And it was the kind ones she pinned her hopes on. Just when Rayne would begin to believe that maybe she could have a normal family with a mommy and daddy that lived in one place and did not travel around so much, the men would suddenly disappear.

Over the years, Rayne had watched her mother use and toss away man after man. And each one had served a purpose. Monique never did anything without purpose. Every affair, every affiliation, every step of her life had been a calculated plan to get ahead. Rayne couldn't help wondering what her mother's original plan had been when she'd betrayed the unsuspecting Katherine.

Even Rayne's birth had been part of a plan, a plan that went awry, but a plan nonetheless. Rayne was meant to be the bait to lure a naive but responsible banker to the altar all in the pursuit of doing the right thing.

It would've worked, too. All Monique's plans worked. But fate had intervened and Rayne's father had died before she ever had a chance to meet him. His small private plane went down off the coast of Maine before he'd ever had a chance to say "I do" to Monique.

Rayne never shared it with anyone, not even Tristan, but she was almost certain her mother would've found a way to get rid of her if she hadn't been eight months pregnant. At that advanced stage, any abortion attempt would've endangered her life, as well.

But it all worked out because Monique found another use for her beautiful child. Meal ticket. Rayne would never forget the first rule she'd made, the when and the where. That first rule had been the beginning of her liberation from Monique and her conniving ways, and it had set the tone for her life. It happened when she was fifteen.

She'd just finished the final shoot for a cereal commercial and the crew was going out to celebrate. Being underage, she'd not been allowed to go, so the stage manager called for her car to take her back to the hotel she was staying in. The car service refused to pick her up, explaining that her last three checks had bounced.

Someone on the commercial set ended up giving her a ride to the hotel. As soon as she could, she called her accountant and discovered that her mother, the so-called guardian of her trust, had emptied her account almost six months prior. Her incompetent accountant swore that he thought she knew. Of course he—like everything else in her life—had been handpicked by Monique.

The next few days Rayne felt as if a veil was being slowly lifted from her eyes. All the misery her mother had caused. Unlike most, Rayne knew that for all her mother's scheming she'd reaped as much as she sowed. Rayne could remember all the times she heard her mother crying in the night. There was something to be said for karma.

Later that week when she returned to Los Angeles and confronted her mother, Monique had shown not even the slightest bit of remorse. Out of everything that was said between the two of them that night, Rayne would never forget her mother's last words to her: "What's the big deal, you'll make more."

Looking back, it seemed like some kind of omen, because that cereal commercial turned out to be her last commercial. In fact, it turned out to be her last acting job.

She had found herself in that awkward stage, somewhere between child and woman, and no one wanted to use her in their ads. She should've been okay because she had a lifetime of income to fall back on. Except the person who was supposed to take care of her and protect her interest had done neither.

Shortly after that, Rayne bought a ticket to New York and never looked back. On the plane ride to New York, she'd come up with her first rule: always control your own money. It was a simple rule and would appear self-evident, but it was a lesson she'd had to learn the hard way and one she would never forget. That day, Rayne Phillips took control of her life and her destiny and she vowed never to surrender it again to anyone.

Somehow, Tristan had made her forget that. He'd gotten under her skin and made her hope for the impossible. He made her want and in the moment she hated him for making her want. He was so beautiful, inside and out. His music was like magic; it touched every part of her being. He understood her on a level that went beyond anything she'd ever experienced. And he was real. She'd never met anyone like that…ever.

Someone so secure in himself that he felt no need to hide any part of himself from people. She loved that most about him, how he opened his heart and invited the world in.

It was such a warm heart, such a comforting place to be. She loved being in his heart. But like everything else, there was a price to be paid. And she was just beginning to understand how high that price would be.

She came upon a music store and stopped when she saw a poster for Optimus Five in the window. Ronnie, Dex, Toby and Steve all giving their best I'm-the-man stances for the photographer.

There in the middle of them stood Tristan, confident Tristan. He didn't need to show the world that he was the man. Anyone looking at him could already see it.

"Sweetheart, are you all right?" An older woman holding an umbrella was staring into her face with a concerned expression.

Rayne looked at the woman briefly, wondering what would cause her to look so troubled. Then glancing back at the poster, she saw her reflection in the store window and fought the urge to burst into laughter.

The mascara on her eyes that she'd neglected to remove the night before was now running, giving her a crazed raccoon look. Her hair plastered to her head looked matted and her clothes were soaked through and through. She looked like a hooker having a bad day.

The woman probably thought she was a derelict because she looked nothing like the successful entrepreneur that she was. The woman proved her suspicion with her next words.

"There's a shelter at fortieth and nine. Would you like to go there?"

Rayne looked back at her reflection and this time she could not stop the laughter that burst from her chest. It was such a wonderful release, and she laughed and laughed, letting all the tension and stress of the morning flow right out of her body.

The woman slowly began backing away from her and by the time Rayne finally got her laughter under control, the woman was gone.

So much for Good Samaritans, she thought. She wiped at her face and only managed to smear the makeup even more, making her look even worse. But that was okay, she decided. Because the laughter had managed to do what nothing else could, she'd finally stopped crying.

With a heavy sigh, she shook her head at the troubled mess of a reflection looking back at her. "If this is love," she spoke to the woman in the glass, "I want no part of it."

Realizing she did not have a purse with her, she checked the pocket of her coat to see if she'd maybe stuck a fell dollar in there as she sometimes did, but it was empty.

With another heavy sigh, she turned and headed back the way she'd come. It took her a minute to get her bearings and troubled her a little that she'd been in such a state that she really had not paid attention to where she was going or her surroundings. No smart New Yorker ever made that mistake.

When she reached her apartment she stopped outside the door, wondering what she would find on the other side. Now, she was more determined than ever to get Tristan out of her life. She was beginning to feel like herself again, the take-control woman that felt as familiar as her skin. And it was time for this relationship to come to an end.

She opened the door thinking she might be greeted by a confrontation, but the apartment was empty. No sign of Tristan. She went into the bedroom and straight to the closet. His two suitcases and few belongings were gone.

She felt slightly guilty knowing he was a stranger in the city and really had nowhere else to go. She wondered if he would try to track down his family and go with them back to Albany.

"Stop it," she scolded herself. "He's a grown man, he'll be all right."

Forcing Tristan from her thoughts, Rayne hurried into the shower and was soon dressed in what she called one of her Marc Jacobs powerful woman outfits, consisting of a black shadow plaid sleeveless shell and matching black slit skirt.

After an hour of blow-drying and curling, her golden locks were back to their usual bounciness. She applied a light coating of makeup and slipped on her favorite gold dragon armlet. Put her small feet into her black Prada sling-back booties, grabbed her Coach bag and was out the door.

She was more sure now than ever that there would be life after Tristan. Her world had not changed so much after all. She could put all the ugliness of that morning behind her and return to the careful existence she'd once valued so highly. Tristan was an anomaly. A once-in-a-lifetime fling, she decided, and every woman deserved one great affair. But that was all it was.

On the cab ride to the club, she spent the time trying to come up with the right words to inform the group that Tristan was no longer a part of them.

As of today, Optimus Five was once again Optimus Four.

They'd survived without him before and they could survive without him again.

She frowned thoughtfully as she stared out the window. Mel might be another problem. She wasn't at all certain she could get him to sign the group without Tristan fronting it. And the guys would not be pleased if her love life ended up costing them this opportunity of a lifetime.

She shook her head sadly. This was why she made a rule of never getting involved with her band members. At that moment, she mentally added a new rule to her list: never break my own rules.

Later that evening, just before opening, Rayne could hear Ronnie and Dex talking as they entered the club. That meant that Steve and Toby would not be far behind.

She stood from her desk where she'd been paying bills, smoothed her blouse and took a deep breath.

*Might as well get this over with.*

She opened the door to her office and started down the hallway toward their dressing room. As she reached the door she could hear the male laughter coming from inside.

She knocked hard and waited until someone answered. The door was cracked and Dex stuck his head out. "Hey, Rayne, what's up?"

"Got a minute? I need to talk to you all together."

"Sure." He opened the door wide and Rayne entered and stopped dead in her tracks to see Tristan leaning against one of the dressing tables. The other four men disappeared as her mind and eyes honed in on the only one that mattered.

"What are you doing here?" The words were out of her mouth before she could stop them.

"I play here, remember?" he said casually, never breaking eye contact with her.

She could feel the other guys watching them and shook

herself free of his hypnotic stare. She glanced around at the others and knew two things instantly.

Dex, Ronnie and Steve had no idea that anything had changed—but Toby did. The guilty expression on his face as he avoided her eyes told her that was where Tristan had landed after leaving her place that morning. She never thought Toby would sell her out like that, but who knew what sad story Tristan had given him.

"Can I talk to you in the hall for a moment?" She returned her attention to Tristan.

"Can it wait? We are trying to get ready for tonight." She glanced at the men again and noticed that none of them seemed too busy, just sitting around and talking from what she could see.

"No, it can't." She turned and headed out the door, never checking to see if he was following. It felt good, too, she thought, being the old Rayne. The take-control Rayne. Tristan had barely gotten a glimpse of this woman before they began their relationship, which had ended in her turning into a pile of wrecked womanhood at his feet.

Well, she thought, it was time he got to know this Rayne better. Once in the hallway, she turned with her hands on her hips. "What do you think you're doing?"

Her eyes widened when she realized she was talking to air; no one else was there.

She was still standing there trying to decide if she should go back into the room and try again or just leave when Tristan finally came into the hall, pulling the door closed behind him.

Before she could speak, he put up his hands in a defensive gesture. "Don't do this."

"Do what?"

"Ruin this band because you have a problem with me."

"I'm not trying to ruin the band, Tristan, but you have to admit it will be a bit awkward working together after everything."

"Not really."

Rayne stood stone still, not certain she'd heard right. "You don't think so?"

"No. I mean I love you, Rayne. True. But my music…my music is my soul. It's the most important thing in the world to me."

*Last night, you said I was the most important thing in the world to you,* she thought.

"I get it. You and me—we're over. I get it. But the music, Rayne…the way we fit together." He gestured to the room behind him. "This doesn't happen every day. You know it as well as I do. Granted, I just got here, and maybe I've been lucky and haven't really had to pay my dues, but these guys have worked hard for a chance, for years they've waited for a record deal like this. Don't take it away from them."

Rayne fought the urge to lean back against the wall. Was he really able to separate the two relationships so easily? Could she? Why had it not occurred to her that they could keep the band together and end their romantic relationship?

In her mind the two things were completely intertwined and you couldn't have one without the other. He'd called her his muse, but apparently a muse was more easily replaceable than she realized. It hurt. It hurt like hell to hear him so easily dismiss what they'd shared. But this was what she wanted, right? No, this was better. This way she could keep access to his wonderful talent without all the emotional entanglements.

"Can you handle that?" he asked.

Rayne looked up into his eyes and saw nothing. That way

he had of always looking at her as if she were some kind of dessert he craved was gone. Now, he was just a man discussing a business venture with his boss. She nodded. "I can handle it if you can."

## Chapter 8

As he strummed his guitar, checking the sound that came out of the amplifier, Tristan wasn't at all sure he could handle this. But it was his only chance, the only way he could stay close to Rayne and fix whatever had gone wrong that morning.

He considered returning to Albany for all of a minute before abandoning the idea. This city was now his home for no other reason than Rayne lived here. And he was determined to find a way to make it right.

So he'd packed his bags and headed to the closest hotel only to find out that a convention in town had booked up not only that one but all the hotels in the area.

The only people he knew in town other than Rayne were the band members, and Ronnie, Dex and Steve were all married with children, which left Toby as the only possible member who might have a spare bed.

The older man had taken him in without so much as a

question, but Tristan knew he'd already figured it out on his own, so there was nothing that needed to be said.

But now, watching the club patrons pour in, watching Rayne do her hostess thing, seeing the way men checked out her beautiful body and knowing that for the first time in several weeks one of them might actually stand a chance with her…this was turning out to be harder than he'd originally imagined.

But he got through it. And the next night and the next. But with every passing day he could feel Rayne pushing him further and further out of her life. And he still had no idea how to undo it. And, God, how he missed her. Her touch, her voice, everything about her. Did she miss him? The only time he seemed to be able to hold her undivided attention was when he was performing.

Living with Toby was proving to be interesting, as well. The man was an absolute neat freak. Everything had to be in a certain spot at all times. He knew that if he continued to stay in New York he could have to consider getting his own place. It was going to be a while before he and Rayne were living together again.

He was playing one of his original songs when Mel came into the club. Mel waved toward the stage before moving through the crowd to reach Rayne. Tristan watched the slick music executive, not liking the way he put his arm around Rayne's shoulders or the way he leaned into her when he spoke.

Tristan continued to play, believing he never missed a beat but something must've happened because Rayne turned to look at him suddenly and he also noticed Toby frowning at him.

Only then did he remember he was supposed to be singing. He quickly filled in the gap and the crowd didn't seem to notice or mind for the most part. The song was upbeat and dancing to the music seemed to be all anyone cared about.

After they finished the set, he quickly put his guitar down and headed down the stairs and offstage, ignoring the cluster of women gathered at the bottom of the stairs. He worked his way over to Rayne and Mel, trying to tap down the growing jealously in his mind.

Mel saw him first. "Hey, man, what's up—forget your lyrics?" He laughed. "Not that this crowd seems to care as long as you continue to jam that bass the way you do."

Tristan forced a smile. "Well, you know. These things happen." He glanced at Rayne.

"Got any news for us?" He heard Dex over his shoulder and realized the whole band had followed him for their own reason, information regarding the deal Mel was working out for them.

"Not yet," Mel said with the shake of his head. "But these things take time."

He glanced nervously at Tristan, and when he was sure, he made a slight head motion indicating the back hall leading to the alley.

Tristan frowned at the man, wondering if he was being called out. But when Mel did it again, he realized he just wanted to talk in private.

"Excuse us a moment," Tristan said. "I need to ask Mel something."

He started to move toward the back of the club and saw Mel start to follow him, then pause. He saw Mel slipping Rayne a card and it took every ounce of his being not to storm back and find out what that was about.

Soon he and Mel were close together in the hallway, right outside the kitchen. As soon as they were alone, Mel began. "We've run into a bit of a snag in the negotiations."

Tristan frowned, wondering why he was the only one being informed of this. "What do you mean?"

"Well, the scouts, they like you—they really do. But that's it."

"I don't understand."

"They only want to sign you, Tristan, not Optimus Five."

"But the demo, the audition, they were all done as a group."

"Doesn't matter. Look, Tristan, I have been coming to this club for years—even before Rayne and I hooked up."

Tristan tightened his jaw. "Get to your point."

Mel looked slightly taken aback but he continued. "We've heard everything those four have to offer. But you…you're new, fresh, exciting. That's what they're looking for. They're has-beens, and you're a yet-to-be. What do you say?"

"Say? To what?"

"Do you want the deal or not?"

"Hang on." Tristan shook his head in disbelief. "Are you telling me the only way I'm going to get a deal is if I stab my partners in the back?"

"A bit over the top, but you've got the gist of it." Mel quickly checked his vibrating phone and returned it to his pocket. "Look, I've got to go, but think about it, okay? You and I both know what this could do for you."

He turned to leave and paused. "By the way, what's going on with you and Rayne?"

"Nothing that concerns you." Tristan could not stop the threatening tone that escaped. Tristan had never really cared for Mel because of his past relationship with Rayne, but now he was beginning to despise the man.

Mel simply smiled. "Just asking." He turned and headed back down the hall leading out of the club. "Oh, and welcome to the club."

"What club?" Tristan called back.

"The Rayne-Phillips-broken-heart club." At the end of the hall, he turned with a wide grin on his face. "I've been a member for years and thought I always would be." He shrugged. "But then again, you just never know what tomorrow will bring."

And he was gone, leaving Tristan alone with nothing but that parting thought.

Unable to stop himself, Tristan went back into the club and immediately began combing the room for Rayne.

When he didn't see her anywhere he started toward her office, but Steve caught his arm. "Come on, man, we're on."

"Start without me," he said, pulling free from the loose hold and continuing in the direction of Rayne's office.

When he reached the office he pounded on the door three times before throwing it open and finding Rayne sitting at her desk. She stood quickly. "What do you think you're doing?"

He took in her elegant black pantsuit and upturned do—no matter how many times he looked at her, it would always feel as if he was seeing someone wonderful and new for the first time. But in his present mood it was hard to appreciate her beauty because all he could think about was the card he'd seen Mel slip into her hand.

"Where is it?" He stormed to the desk and began pushing things to the side trying to find the small card.

"What are you talking about?" Rayne watched him in amazement.

"Where is what? The card Mel gave you. What's on it?"

Her eyes narrowed. "None of your damn business! Now get out of my office!" She tilted her head to the side as she listened to the music coming from the main area. "Aren't you supposed to be onstage right now?"

Tristan continued to push aside the papers until he was satisfied it was not there. "Where is it?"

"What is wrong with you?" She frowned thoughtfully. "What did Mel say to you?"

"Where is the card, Rayne?" She folded her arms across her chest and simply glared at him. "I saw him give it to you. What was on it? His phone number?"

"I already have his phone number, you dweeb! We're business partners, remember?"

"Did he ask you out? Did you make plans to meet him somewhere? Is that what was on the card? An address?"

She shook her head. "I've never seen you like this."

"Get used to it," he muttered.

"I knew this would never work."

Tristan took a deep breath. "I just want to see the card. Let me see it and then I'll leave, okay?"

"No."

"Woman," he growled low in his throat, "give me the damn card!"

He began looking around the room. His eyes came back to her face just in time to notice her guilty glance toward her purse sitting on the corner chaise.

When their eyes met, Rayne realized she'd given herself away and they both charged at the purse at the same time.

She reached it first, but barely.

Rayne had spoken the truth, she'd never seen Tristan like this. He'd always been a passionate lover, but in most ways he seemed so self-contained. She would've never imagined him in a jealous rage and she was sure that was exactly what this was.

The card was nothing more than a new business card for Mel. He'd moved offices and changed phone numbers and he was handing out new cards to all his acquaintances, but apparently Tristan thought it was a lot more.

Tugging over the purse, the pair tripped and fell to the

couch. Rayne had managed to get the purse beneath her but she was having a hard time holding on to it.

Mostly because the feel of Tristan's warm body on top of her own was far too distracting. She wanted nothing more than to wrap her arms around his neck and pull his lips to hers, but he was still completely intent on the purse.

His strong arms wrapped around her body, his muscular legs weighing her down, his hot breath on her neck, it was all so wonderful and in that moment she wanted to thank Mel for the inconsequential act that had given her this moment. A moment she thought she would never experience again, even if the true purpose of the contact was possession of her purse.

Suddenly, he stopped squirming and reaching, and Rayne was afraid he was about to give up. But instead he propped himself up on his elbows and looked down at her. His heavy breathing had changed. His eyes had darkened to a deep brown as they roamed over her heaving breast. She tried to regain control of her own erratic breathing, but it was no good with him looking at her like that. It had been so long since he'd looked at her like that.

The room grew quiet in the wake of their struggle and Rayne had no idea what he was thinking until he spoke the thought in three words.

"I want you."

# Chapter 9

*Okay,* Rayne thought. This was where she was supposed to remember her rule about never returning to the same metaphoric well to quench thirst. But how could she not when the water in this particular well was so damn good?

Without a word she released her tight hold on the purse buried under her back to cup his face in her hands. Slowly, with precision and clear intent, she brought his lips to hers.

Rayne never wanted either of them to say this just happened. Nothing between them would ever just happen. That was important, she wasn't exactly sure why at that moment, but it was.

She felt Tristan's large hand wrapping around her bottom, lifting her legs over his hips. The slick fabric of her pants sliding along his thigh seemed to increase his arousal as she felt his penis growing against her stomach.

His other hand eased up to cup her breast beneath the silk blouse, and she spontaneously arched into him. Wanting him—no, needing him as she'd never needed anything. It was such a strange revelation, Rayne thought. Like a starving man who does not know he's starving until he tastes food. An awakening in some ways.

Charting a path from her lips and down her neck, he replaced the hand massaging her breast with his mouth and Rayne grabbed his shoulders, trying to hang on to something resembling control as he suckled hard.

"I want you," he whispered in her ear, as if to confirm any doubt she may have had before returning to the breast that was already craving his attention.

With quick work, he had the blouse unbuttoned and off her shoulders. With the flip of his fingers her front-latching bra was open, exposing her brown mounds to him.

And he dove in with a zestfulness that caused her to laugh out loud. The laughter soon turned to a moan of satisfaction as he pulled first one and then the other breast into his mouth.

Rayne could hold back no longer; soon she was ripping his shirt off his shoulders, needing to feel his skin against hers, and he was eager to help her. He sat up and pulled the spandex material of the costume over his head.

She reached for the button fly of his jeans and tugged hard but nothing happened. He smiled, a smile of pure seduction, as he slowly released the buttons and pulled the jeans down over his hips along with his underwear. "Is this what you want?" he asked, stroking his hand over his penis. Rayne gently reached out to touch him.

Yes, she thought, it was exactly what she wanted. Taking his manhood into her hands, she stroked him, watching the expressions of both pleasure and pain pass over his face.

It had been so long all she wanted was to touch him, to feel his skin against hers, but that simple pleasure was cut short as Tristan quickly stood and removed his jeans.

He rummaged in his pocket a moment and came up with

a condom. Donning it quickly, he covered her body with his and then he was entering her.

Rayne wrapped her arms around his chest and held on with all her strength, never wanting to lose this feeling again. His lips found hers and with a kiss and their bodies they told each other what words never could.

Rayne felt as if the world were spinning around her. No one, nothing, had ever been like it was with Tristan. The level of intensity he brought out in her still stunned her. For so long, she had worked to control her emotions, learned to minimize a person's effect on her. She gave only what she wanted to give and took only what she needed to take. But with Tristan the lines had become blurred. The want was endless and the need was all-consuming. He was not just her lover, he was her addiction.

And at that moment, she was as lost to his touch as a recovering alcoholic would be with that first sip. Lost…lost… lost.

Holding to him with all her strength did nothing to stop the tidal wave of pleasure that coursed through her body as she gave up her woman's nectar.

She felt Tristan bury his head against her neck as his arms tightened around her thighs and he gave in to his own release.

When she opened her eyes a few minutes later it was to find Tristan sitting beside her on the sofa in his jeans. He was holding his costume shirt in his hands as he watched her nap.

"Hey there, sleeping beauty," he whispered as he leaned forward to kiss her forehead.

Rayne yawned and sat up, surprised to find she had fallen asleep.

"I need to get back out there before they realize how good

they sound without me." He smiled as he gestured to the door. "Can we talk later?" he asked, pulling the shirt over his head.

She nodded, not sure what else to say. Then with another quick peck on the forehead he was gone.

Rayne sat up on the couch and, feeling the fabric against her bare skin, suddenly remembered she was naked. She quickly stood and redressed hoping no one came looking for her too soon. She flopped down on the couch, realizing she'd just broken another of her rules. She'd never made love in her office before. She'd said from the beginning of the club that her office was for business only. *So much for that,* she thought.

She knew the exact moment Tristan retook the stage because of the roar of the crowd. Despite whatever was going on between them, there was no denying Tristan Daniels had been good for Optimus.

She stood again and picked up her battered purse. "All that fighting and he still didn't get the card," she muttered with a shake of her head.

No matter how she tried, she could not concentrate for the rest of the evening. Normally she went out and mixed with the crowd throughout the night, but instead she huddled in her office trying to make sense of what had happened.

For so many years, sex had just been a thing she did. It was a physical release, an exercise of sorts, and if her partner happened to be good at it all the better. It was just sex.

But no matter how she tried, she could not place what had just happened in that category. She wanted to. She desperately wanted to. She wanted to be able to bed Tristan whenever the mood struck—and the mood struck quite often. But in her heart of hearts she knew it would never be that way between them.

She placed her elbows on the table and propped her chin in her hands and finally admitted the truth to herself. For the first time in her life, Rayne Phillips had fallen in love. With a twenty-four-year-old bass-playing schoolteacher no less! What the hell?

As she listened to the band play, she considered what Tristan wanted to talk about. She already knew. She decided it had to be a side effect of being in love. People in love could apparently read each other's minds.

He would want to move back in with her. He would want to pick up where they left off. He would want to make peace between his family and her. He would want—no, expect to have a normal, healthy committed relationship.

The problem was that Rayne had no idea of what that was. She'd heard about it; she'd even seen some couples who managed to pull it off. But the details were sketchy.

For instance, how did a woman manage to feel what she felt for Tristan and keep from giving him too much control over her life? And her hard-won control was not something she was willing to give up easily. Not even for Tristan.

And the pain of losing him…

The past few days had been some of the hardest of her life. She wasn't quite sure she could go through that again. So what were her options?

The sound of Tristan's voice came through the walls as he sang "Beats of My Heart"—and Rayne knew he was playing it just for her. He was speaking to her through the walls, over the heads of the crowd. Even now, surrounded by his adoring fans, he was reaching out to her. What woman wouldn't love a man like that?

The stress of trying to decide how to move forward combined with their rambunctious lovemaking had her yawning and she decided to lay her head on the desk just for a few minutes to take a short nap.

She awoke four hours later to find Tristan sitting across from her desk, just watching her sleep.

When he saw her eyes open, he smiled. "Wow, I must've really put it on you, huh?"

She twisted her mouth in a sarcastic expression. "Don't flatter yourself. I just haven't been sleeping well."

His smile faded slightly. "Me either."

Glancing at her desk clock, she saw it was fifteen minutes past two in the morning. "I can't believe I slept so long."

Tristan reached forward and picked up her glass paperweight. "It's okay, I closed the club. Everyone's gone except us." His face had taken on a solemn expression. He tossed the paperweight casually. "So?"

She looked at him and considered pleading ignorance, but he deserved better than that. "I don't know."

"What am I missing, Rayne?" He leaned forward, returning the paperweight to the desk. "I feel like there is a barrier between us that only you can see. It's frustrating. How can I knock down a wall I can't see?"

"Maybe it's not meant to be knocked down?"

"Is that what you think?"

"I don't know." She shook her head in frustration. "This is all new to me."

"How about we take it a day at a time?"

"What's that supposed to mean?"

"Don't rush things, just take it nice and slow. Go back to the way it was before my family showed up."

"I don't think I can do that either."

He chuckled. "You are the most infuriating woman I've ever met."

"Tristan, I like my life the way it is. I've been quite satisfied with it until now. What you want is so different from anything I know, I'm not sure how to deal with it."

"You don't even know what I want."

"Yes, I do."

"What would that be, Rayne?"

"You want a committed relationship."

He tilted his head to the side. "Would you find it that hard to be faithful?"

"Commitment is more than being faithful, and you know it."

"Look, I'm not asking you to wear a chastity belt or tattoo my name on your forehead. But, yes, I do want some kind of commitment."

"And when I start feeling like a caged animal. Then what?"

"Why would you feel like a caged animal?"

She simply stared at him for several long seconds before shaking her head in denial. "Never mind, bad choice of words."

"No, tell me. Why would you feel that way?"

"I like being in control of my own life, Tristan. You give that up in a relationship."

"Where do you get this crazy nonsense?" He frowned. "I thought our problem had something to do with you not wanting to settle for one man. But this is a lot bigger than that. You're afraid of sharing yourself with someone."

"Sharing myself?"

"Opening up to someone."

"We open up to each other all the time."

"No, you tell me about your past and I tell you about mine. I'm talking about something totally different. I'm talking about the future. I'm talking about sharing the future."

She frowned at him. "You know what," she said as she stood from her chair, "it's late. Way too late for this. I'm going home. Let's have this discussion when I'm fresh." She pushed her chair in to the desk. "Are you coming home with me?"

He stood staring into her eyes. "I don't think so." He looked away. "I need to think, something I don't do well when I'm with you."

He regretted the words when he saw the slightly hurt expression that quickly passed over her face. She shrugged in false indifference. "Suit yourself." She collected her purse. "Can you lock up when you leave?"

He nodded and watched as she dropped the ring of keys for the club on the desk in front of him and without so much as a backward glance walked out of the office.

The next morning, Tristan was walking to his post office box to collect his mail when his cell phone rang. "Hello?"

"Hey, man, what's up?" Mel Ferrell's voice came through the line.

Tristan frowned slightly, wondering how Mel had gotten his cell phone number. "What do you need, Mel?"

"Have you thought about my offer?"

"What offer?"

"The solo album we discussed last night."

Tristan had completely forgotten about their discussion in the hallway. "Solo album?"

"Man, that woman has you all twisted in knots. Pay attention this time. My label wants to sign you, just you—not Optimus Four. Now, do you have a problem with that?"

Tristan stopped walking. "Hell, yeah, I have a problem with that. No deal. It's all or nothing."

"Before you go all musketeer on me, think about it, because this is the last time I will be making this offer. There are fifty guys standing in line behind you dying for a chance like this. Now, I know you feel loyalty to those guys, but let's be real. How long have you really known them? A few weeks? You don't owe them anything."

Tristan let his eyes float over the people rushing by him in all directions while he considered the offer. What Mel Ferrell was offering was a devil's deal. But he would've been lying to himself if he pretended it was not a tempting offer. Then again, the devil's deals usually were.

What Mel was offering was exactly what he'd come to New York seeking—or so he thought. Now he realized he would've been just as happy spending the rest of his days performing at the Optimus, as long as he could have Rayne by his side while he did it. But at this point, he couldn't even be certain of that future.

"Can I have some time to think about it?"

"Take all the time you want. But I need an answer by tomorrow. Like I said, there are others we are considering, as well."

After he ended his call with Mel, Tristan continued to the post office and then headed to a nearby greasy spoon for breakfast. As he sat in a back booth of the small restaurant, his mind was racing with recent events.

The world had changed so much since he'd come to New York. A part of him was wishing he'd just stayed in Albany, and continued to dream. "Be careful what you wish for," he muttered to himself.

"What's that, sweetie?" His waitress appeared at his side. She was a middle-aged woman of average appearance.

He lifted his coffee cup. "Can I get a refill?"

She poured the coffee and noticed the notes he was scribbling on a napkin. "What's that?"

He glanced down at the paper. "I'm a songwriter."

Her eyes lit up. "Really? Are you famous?"

He smiled. "Not yet."

Her face twisted in thought, then she quickly reached over and grabbed another napkin. "Can I get your autograph anyway? Just in case."

Tristan couldn't stop the laugh that escaped. "Why not?"

He quickly signed his name on the napkin and the waitress

tucked it into her pocket. "Thanks. Who knows, one day this may be worth something."

"Who knows?"

She continued on to the next table and Tristan was once again left alone with his thoughts. He continued to stare out the window until finally…it came to him like an epiphany. He knew what he needed to do.

He pulled a fresh napkin to him and began to write.

# Chapter 10

As he entered the club that night, he was running late. The club was already jumping with patrons and the evening was well under way.

As he hurried down the hallway, Tristan could hear commotion coming from the dressing room. As soon as he opened the door all sound ceased.

Dex, Ronnie, Toby and Steve, who all seemed to have been huddled together in deep discussion, turned and looked at him with solemn expressions.

Tristan knew instantly that Mel Ferrell's offer had somehow become public knowledge.

"What's up, fellas?" he asked, coming into the room and closing the door behind him.

Dex stepped away from the group. "Okay, let's get all the awkward stuff out of the way. No one here blames you, Tristan."

"Blames me for what?"

"We know Mel offered you the contract," Ronnie spoke up. "Only you."

"Nobody blames you for taking it," Steve said.

"Who said I took it?" he asked, moving to the closet to collect a clean costume shirt. The one he wore the night before still smelled like Rayne.

The other men each looked at each other. Dex stepped forward again. "Tristan, you have to take it. You can't pass up a chance like this."

Tristan found a shirt that would fit and pulled it out of the closet before turning back to the group. "Watch me."

Toby stepped through the group and walked up to him. "I like you, Tristan, but if it were me I would take it." He gestured to the others. "Any of us would've."

Dex placed his hand on Tristan's shoulder in a show of support. "We all knew you were going places the first time we heard you sing. This really doesn't surprise any of us. So don't feel like you're betraying us. This is your moment—go for it."

"Look, I appreciate all the support." Tristan moved away from the group and quickly changed shirts. "But I've already made up my mind. I'm going back to Albany."

Without warning, the dressing-room door swung open and Rayne stood there with wide, frightened eyes. "You're going back to Albany. But why?"

Seeing the startled expression on the faces of the others, Tristan quickly crossed the room and guided her by the arm back into the hallway, pulling the door closed behind him.

Rayne quickly turned to face him. "Why? I thought—after last night…"

Tristan placed his hand over her lips. "Don't say anything." He reached inside his pants pocket and pulled out the folded napkin. "Just read this." He handed her the napkin, and, taking her by the shoulders, turned her in the direction of her office.

"I admit," he said, giving her a gentle push, "I'm too much of a coward to watch you read it, so take it back to your office."

"What is this?"

"Just read it." He placed a gentle kiss on the back of her head, taking the time to breathe in her perfume, knowing he may not have many more opportunities like this. And then he disappeared back into the dressing room.

As soon as he was gone, Rayne opened the napkin and something fell out onto the floor. She quickly bent to pick it up and her breath caught in her throat. She stood slowly, not believing what she was looking at.

*The yellow diamond from the store window!* But now it was set in a gold ring and surrounded by various colored precious stones. Needing to sit down, she remembered where she was and hurried down the hall to her office.

She flopped down in her desk chair and reopened the napkin. The solitaire diamond sparkled in the bright office light, and, looking at it, Rayne realized how well Tristan understood her nature. The ring was exactly what she would've chosen for herself. Looking at the napkin again, she saw it had two simple words scribbled on it: "Marry me."

That was it, the two words and the diamond ring. Her heart sped up. Was he insane? How could he just spring this on her like this? And he didn't even have the decency to do it in person.

It took everything in her not to go back to that dressing room right now and give him a piece of her mind! Just then, the diamond caught a ray of light and the beauty of the stone was revealed. Her heart softened.

In all the so-called relationships she'd experienced in her adult life, Rayne could not remember any one of them ending in a marriage proposal. Primarily because the men she dated were not the marrying kind, nor did she give off the vibe that she would be responsive to such a request.

But, like everything else about her relationship with Tristan, this did not follow the standard guidelines. He wanted to marry her. He wanted a committed relationship all right, Rayne thought. You don't get much more committed than that.

Then a cold chill ran down her spine as she remembered what she'd heard when she'd been eavesdropping at the door. Like the others, she had heard of Mel's offer, as well, and was eager to see how Tristan was handling it.

But she'd just heard him say he was going back to Albany. Did that mean he thought she would be going with him? Did he honestly think she would just give up her club and follow him to some small upstate town?

No, he couldn't possibly expect that. Could he? She stood from her desk. They definitely needed to talk. But before she even reached the door, she heard the crowd roar as the band took the stage and she knew she'd missed her chance. She would have to wait until they came off the stage again.

As the evening went on, Rayne became more and more restless. She went out into the club and greeted her guests, but her eyes kept returning to the stage and the handsome front man who was watching her with equal attention.

Her mind kept trying to wrap around the idea of being Tristan's wife. The idea of sharing their lives, together, forever. But after a lifetime of conditioning herself to reject even the suggestion of marriage, it was hard to finally accept that maybe she'd found the one man with whom she could make it work.

For the first time, she broke her own rule of not drinking while she was working and helped herself to a glass of claret from behind the bar. It had just the calming effect she wanted.

She sat at the end of the bar enjoying her drink and watching the band play, and she was starting to think she could make it through the night. Then Tristan raised the stakes in their little game of love and with a few poorly chosen words shot her nice little buzz all to hell.

"This next song is about a very special lady." He quietly strummed his guitar and the band picked up the chord and joined in as he played the beginning of "Beats of My Heart."

"She's the light of my world…my beating heart." He continued to play as his eyes found Rayne's. "She's my everything."

Rayne's eyes widened as she realized he was announcing their relationship to everyone in the club. So much for professionalism.

"And," Tristan continued, "tonight I asked her to be my wife."

The crowd went wild as he played the song and it became apparent who he was talking about. Heads began to turn and Rayne tried to ignore the stinging sensation in her brain, as even the band members seemed to look at her differently.

How could he? Rayne stood and hurried back to her office. She stormed in and slammed the door shut, not realizing the music coming from the club had changed.

A second later the door opened again and Tristan stood there. "Rayne?"

She spun around, still raging from the embarrassment he'd just caused her. "How dare you?"

He closed the door behind him. "What?"

"How dare you announce our relationship to the whole world? This may be a nightclub, but it is still a business!"

"What are you getting so angry about? It's not like I gave your answer."

"You had no right!"

"Rayne, I think you are overreacting."

"Am I?" She picked up the ring and threw it at him. "How's that for overreacting! Now take it and get the hell out!"

Tristan looked down to where the ring had fallen at his feet and then back up at the woman whom he'd offered it to.

Without another word, he bent and picked up the ring and then turned and walked out of the office, closing the door behind him.

Fifteen minutes later, when Rayne finally calmed down, the impact of what she'd just done reached her brain. Covering her mouth with both hands, she sat down in her chair. "Oh, God, what have I done?"

A week later, Tristan was back in Albany, sitting down to have dinner with his family at his parents' house. It was one of the quietest meals they'd had in years.

Everyone seemed afraid to ask what had brought him back to Albany so suddenly, but he knew their curiosity was burning.

He was thinking about the fact that before leaving for New York, his family had often eaten together. Just the five of them—his parents, Tracy and Calvin and himself. But somewhere in the back of his mind, Tristan had always expected there to be a sixth person added to the family meals. He'd always planned to marry.

He glanced at the clock again, and considered where Rayne would be at this time of the evening. Probably at the club, in her office.

"I saw Chad earlier today," Kate cut into his thoughts. "He said you reapplied for your position at the school."

Tristan nodded. "The new school year will be starting in a few weeks and he hadn't filled my position yet."

The table fell silent again as even Tracy seemed at a loss

for words. The clanking of silverware filled the void, but it could do nothing for the tension in the air.

"Are you going to go back to playing local clubs?" Calvin asked, seeming desperate to have something to say.

"Maybe," Tristan muttered. "I'm not sure yet."

He ate a little more, but it was becoming obvious to him that he was the reason for the discomfort. He wiped his mouth and stood.

"I'm going to get going."

"So soon?" Kate asked, reaching out to touch his hand.

"Yeah, I still have some unpacking to do. The storage unit I kept it in apparently flooded and some of my stuff got messed up. I need to fill out the damage report before it's too late."

"Sorry to hear that, son," Ben said.

"Thanks, Dad." He gently pulled his hand from his mother's. "Good night, everyone." He turned and headed to the front door. As soon as he was out on the porch in the fresh air he felt as if he could breathe again.

He understood what they were feeling, but didn't know how to make it any better. Truth of the matter was that he was mourning. He was mourning as surely as if someone had died. He'd lost something very important to him. And there was nothing to be done but to let it run its course. It took a man time to come to grips with losing the love of his life.

Feeling the cool air of the early autumn evening, he blew on his hands and headed down the stairs to his car. There was a slight upside to coming home, he'd found. Where New York was a walking town, the people of Albany had no shame in using cars to get around. And he had all his stuff back, even if some of it was slightly damaged. There was some comfort in being surrounded by his own things. As he climbed into his car and started it up, he hoped now his family would be able to enjoy the rest of the meal in his absence.

## Chapter 11

As Tristan pulled away from the curb, Kate let the curtain fall back in place where she'd been looking out at him. She straightened her spine and turned to her family with a solemn expression. "We did this."

"What?"

"Huh?"

"Uh-uh."

Confused responses came from the table, as they each denied responsibility in their own way. But she knew they all understood. Their little surprise trip to New York had ruined her son's relationship.

No, Kate forced herself to be honest. It wasn't the trip, it was her reaction at seeing the daughter of Monique Phillips cuddled against Tristan's side. In her mind, it was like watching her baby boy cuddle up with a snake. But he loved that snake. That much was now painfully obvious.

"Did he say what happened?" Ben asked.

Kate shook her head. "He won't talk about it."

"Well, I say good riddance to bad rubbish." Tracy added, "That woman was nothing but trouble."

"But, it's pretty obvious he was serious about her," Calvin said.

"She probably used him and dumped him. She had that look about her," Tracy said.

Kate thought about that for a moment. That sounded like something Monique would do and she couldn't help but wonder was daughter like mother?

Her son was trying to rebuild his life when it was so obvious he was devastated by whatever had happened between them, and *that woman* was probably going on with her life as if nothing had happened.

She listened to the table conversation that was now flowing freely, as the restriction of Tristan's presence had been removed. Her mind was working; she wanted Rayne Phillips to know that she couldn't just go around breaking hearts without concern for the consequences. She had not been able to stop Monique Phillips from trampling over everyone and everything in her path, but damn if she couldn't stop the next generation!


Kate stood outside the nightclub, wondering if she could go through with this. Of all the women for him to fall in love with…Monique's *daughter*.

"The heart wants what the heart wants," she muttered out loud. She pulled the door open and entered the club and a feeling of familiarity rushed over her. It had been a long time since she'd been in a place like this, but once upon a time clubs like Optimus had been home.

No one was around, but she could hear music coming from somewhere in the distance. "Hello?"

When no one answered, she moved toward the bar farther

into the light. "Hello? Anyone here?" she called again, but no answer. She glanced at her watch. It was six o'clock, so where was the staff?

She walked down a long hallway lined with pictures of the club during its creation. She stopped and just stood staring at one that had Rayne smiling at the camera as she lifted a paintbrush.

Kate shook her head again, still amazed that the girl looked so much like her mother. She had suffered such humiliation at the hands of Monique Phillips, and now her son was a victim of the daughter. The Phillips women were apparently a pack of vipers, destroying everything and everyone they touched.

One look at those pictures and anyone could see what a proud, arrogant creature Rayne Phillips was. Would she even care that Tristan was hurting? And if she didn't care, could Kate handle her indifference without slapping her silly?

She had not come for a fight; she'd come to let this young woman know what she'd done. But now, she was thinking that maybe this trip was a bad idea. Maybe she should just leave now, before it was too late.

No, she decided. Even if the younger woman showed no concern, she wanted her to know how her shallow actions had destroyed a life. She continued along the hallway until she came to a door that simply said "Rayne."

She knocked and heard some commotion behind the door before a soft voice finally said, "Come in."

Kate straightened her back, prepared herself for battle, opened the door and was completely shocked by what she saw. The woman sitting behind the desk was not the proud, regal woman staring back at her from the photos on the walls. This woman was in as bad shape as her son.

Rayne wiped her red nose and looked up with wide eyes to see Kate Daniels standing in her doorway. Quickly her eyes darted past the woman hoping to see... But he wasn't there.

Her eyes returned to Kate as confusion came over her. "What are you doing here?" Rayne asked the question before she realized it. *Tristan's mother?*

She wiped at her nose again and tried to pull herself together, but it was useless. She looked like she felt, a complete mess. She hadn't stopped crying in the five days since he'd left, and it did not seem as if she could get a reprieve even as this woman who despised her stood in the doorway.

Kate Daniels stood in the door with a slight frown on her face. "I'm not sure anymore." Slowly, she moved into the room until she was standing behind one of the plush red chairs that faced the desk. "I came here to give you a piece of my mind for breaking my son's heart, but, frankly, you look even worse than he does."

Rayne tried to fight down the burst of hope she felt in her chest, but she knew it still escaped through her eyes as she took in the words. "What do you mean?"

Kate smirked. "I think you know. But why?" She came around the chair and sat down. "If you're both so damn miserable apart, why did you part in the first place?"

Rayne had no answer for the question. None of the justifications she gave herself the day he left meant anything anymore.

Kate's expression turned thoughtful. "I want to apologize. I know I was kind of hard on you before. It's just seeing you caught me by surprise. It was wrong of me to hold you responsible for the things your mother did."

Rayne simply shrugged. "It's okay. I'm used to it. It feels like I've been paying for her crimes my whole life."

"Do you mind if I ask what happened between you two? Tristan won't talk about it."

Rayne nodded knowingly. "Then please understand, I have to respect his wishes."

Kate sighed. "Fine. I guess I have to leave it at that." She glanced around the room. "Well, this is awkward. I came down here to give you a piece of my mind for hurting my son, but it looks as if you were hurt just as bad."

Rayne swiped at her running nose with her tissue, but said nothing else. Kate's words were an understatement. The pain she was feeling in her soul at that moment went so far beyond hurt, there was no way to describe it.

"Tell me this much. Why haven't you called him?"

Rayne looked directly at the older woman. "Why hasn't he called me?"

"Oh—good Lord!" Kate threw up her hands in surrender. "Is that what's going on here? Some kind of stupid standoff?"

Rayne shook her head. "No, we just both realized we wanted different things."

"Really? Because from where I sit it looks as if you both want exactly the same thing. To be together."

Rayne's eyes narrowed. "You should know better than anyone that Tristan needs to be with someone else. Someone less toxic. I'm Monique Phillips's daughter, remember? In the end, I would only destroy him the way my mother destroyed everything she touched."

Kate was startled by the venomous statement. "You're her daughter, Rayne. You're not her. Your life will be whatever you make it."

"You don't understand."

Kate stood. "I guess not. Because there is no way in hell anything would've kept me from spending my life with Ben." She turned to leave. "Since both of you seem to be equally stubborn, I have no idea how to help you. I really wish I could, though." With that, she quietly walked out, pulling the door closed behind her.

Rayne sat staring at the closed door for several minutes, thinking about the woman's words. She pulled a new tissue from the box and tossed out the old. She glanced at the trash can slightly surprised to see it was full of her worn-out tissues.

Was it really that simple? Could just wanting to be together be enough? She quickly stood from her chair, grabbed up her purse and keys and rushed to the door.

"Mrs. Daniels! Wait for me!"

Tristan was sitting at his desk in the empty classroom writing out his lesson plan when the door opened. He glanced up and his heart stopped.

At first he thought his imagination was playing tricks on him, but the vision before him did not change. He stood from his chair slowly, still fearful that any sudden move might end the fantasy.

"Rayne?" he asked, wanting to believe she was real.

She stared at him with a small smile for several seconds before turning to look around the room. "Been a long time since I was in a high-school classroom."

Tristan swallowed hard. "What are you doing here?"

She glanced at him over her shoulder. "Your mom came to see me."

"What?"

She walked over to the window and looked out. "She said you were miserable without me."

"I am," Tristan said, his eyes narrowing in on her back. "But, then again, I told you I would be. It didn't seem to make a difference."

She glanced at him again. "Do you like it here?"

"Rayne, what are you doing here?"

She turned and braced her weight on the windowsill. "I don't know."

Tristan started across the room to her. "Sure about that?"

"I've never done the long-term thing, Tristan. I don't know if I'm built for it."

"That's your problem. You keep thinking of *us* as a thing. We're not a thing, Rayne. This is not some fling, or short-term affair or even friendship with benefits. This is the real deal."

"Love?"

"There is no imitating it. And…there is no escaping it."

"I've never been in love."

"Neither have I."

"Aren't you scared? What if we don't make it?"

"What if we do?"

She placed her hand over her heart. "For the past five days I have felt empty in here. It hurt so bad, Tristan. I don't want to hurt like that again."

He closed the distance between them. "Don't think about that. Think about how it felt when we were together. Remember that feeling? We can have that feeling all the time, Rayne."

He took her hands in his. "What it comes down to, Rayne, is vulnerability. In love, you're vulnerable—that's just a fact. But I can promise you that if you spend your life with me, I will make sure you never *feel* vulnerable."

"How can you promise that?"

"Because every day I will remind you how much I love you, how complete you make me, how right we are together. I will assure you every morning that you are just where you're supposed to be—in my arms. And I will write song after song to remind you of how much I love you."

"I'm scared."

"I know. You have no reason to believe me, no reason to trust me. Everyone you've ever trusted has betrayed you. But I won't, Rayne. And only time will prove that."

She looked down to where their hands were connected. "I've missed you so much."

Tristan pulled her into his arms. "Not any more than I've missed you."

Rayne wrapped her arms around his neck, feeling relief flood her whole being. She'd almost lost him. She'd almost missed out on *her* opportunity of a lifetime. All because she was allowing the past to control her future.

"I love you," she whispered in his ear.

"I know." He kissed her neck. "And I pledge to spend the rest of my life reminding you of why."

As his lips closed over hers, Rayne felt the ghost of Monique that she'd carried around for a lifetime simply floating away, leaving only Rayne.

She leaned back to see his face. "What now?"

His handsome face spread to a wide grin. "I thought you'd never ask. Let's go back to my place."

She frowned in annoyance. "No, I mean where do we go from here?"

"That depends on you." He released her long enough to reach up around his neck and pull a chain from beneath his shirt.

Rayne gasped and covered her mouth, realizing that dangling from the chain was the yellow diamond engagement ring he'd given her before.

"I believe this belongs to you." He took the ring off the chain and gently placed it in the palm of her hand. "Whenever you're ready to wear it."

She looked up at him unable to hide the tears in her eyes. "But...why?" She looked at the ring in her palm and back to the man she loved. "Why did you hold on to it?"

He shrugged. "I don't know. I guess some part of me still believed."

Rayne was too stunned to do anything but stand staring at the ring.

Tristan lifted her chin until they were eye to eye once more. "So, Rayne, where do you want to go from here?"

Rayne bit her bottom lip, considering. She didn't want to

spoil the perfect moment but she needed to know where he stood on a certain issue. "Would you be willing to move back to New York?"

"Yes, I know how much Optimus means to you. But, Rayne...when we start having children I would like you to at least consider moving back to Albany."

Her eyes widened. "Children?"

His smile fell as sadness entered his eyes. "You don't want children?"

She smiled. "I never thought about it."

He placed another quick kiss on her lips. "Well, think about it. Personally, I would like to have at least one."

She cupped his face in her hands. "A little Tristan."

"Or a little Rayne."

Her expression turned thoughtful. "A baby," she whispered in awe.

Tristan smiled, seeing the wistfulness she had no idea was reflected in her eyes. "Just think about it. We have time."

She quickly slipped the diamond ring on her finger and huffed loudly. "Maybe you do, but my biological clock is ticking. I'm almost thirty, remember?"

He took her hand and headed toward the door with the intention of taking her back to his apartment. "Well, then, we don't have a moment to waste."

\* \* \* \* \*

# REQUEST YOUR FREE BOOKS!

## 2 FREE NOVELS
## PLUS 2 FREE GIFTS!

**KIMANI ROMANCE**

### Love's ultimate destination!

KROM10